ENTERTAINING
Distraction

DOMS OF THE COVENANT BOOK 2

SAMANTHA COLE

Entertaining Distraction
Copyright ©2017 Samantha A. Cole
All Rights Reserved.
Published by Suspenseful Seduction Publishing.

Editing by Eve Arroyo—www.evearroyo.com

Entertaining Distraction is a work of fiction. Names, characters, businesses, organizations, places, events, and incidents either are the product of the author's imagination or are used fictitiously. Any resemblance to actual persons, living or dead, events, or locales is entirely coincidental.

No part of this book may be reproduced or used in any manner without the express written permission of the publisher except for the use of brief quotations in a book review. This ebook is licensed for your personal enjoyment only. This book may not be re-sold or given away to other people. If you would like to share this ebook with another person, please purchase an additional copy for each recipient. If you're reading this book and did not purchase it, or it was not purchased for your use only, then please return to your favorite ebook retailer and purchase your own copy. Thank you for respecting the hard work of this author.

To the Sexy Six-Pack's Sirens!

Acknowledgments

To the Sexy Six-Pack's Sirens group—it was a pleasure to dedicate this book to you. I know you've waited a long time for Mistress China to get her story. I hope I did her justice in your eyes.

To my beta readers—Allena, Ame, Angi, Cathy, Charla, Debbie, Elizabeth, Felisha, Jen, Joanne, Katie, Milynn, Olivia, Rhonda, Susan, and Tawnya—thank you for all your input and continued support.

To Milynn—thank you for helping me find Mistress China's voice. This story wouldn't be the same without your input.

To my editor Eve—one of these days I'll get a deadline right!

To my PAs, Connie and Maria—you ladies are the best! To Kelle, Brandie, Jules, and Jess—love ya lots!

To Nancy Walker and Susan Kelly—two of my readers who'd won the opportunity to have characters named after them. Ladies, you're mentioned in here briefly but don't be surprised if you show up in another book! (I can guarantee you will!)

And as always, thank you to my readers for loving my stories and characters as much as I love writing them!

Author's Note

The story within these pages is completely fictional but the concepts of BDSM are real. If you do choose to participate in the BDSM lifestyle, please research it carefully and take all precautions to protect yourself. Fiction is based on real life but real life is *not* based on fiction. Remember—Safe, Sane and Consensual!

History of Trident Security & The Covenant

***While not every character is in every book, these are the ones with the most mentions throughout the series. This guide will help keep readers straight about who's who.

Trident Security (TS) is a private investigative and military agency, co-owned by Ian and Devon Sawyer. With governmental and civilian contracts, the company got its start when the brothers and a few of their teammates from SEAL Team Four retired to the private sector. The original six-man team is referred to as the Sexy Six-Pack, as they were dubbed by Kristen Sawyer, née Anders, or the Alpha Team. Trident had since expanded and former members of the military and law enforcement have been added to the staff. The company is located on a guarded compound, which was a former import/export company cover for a drug trafficking operation in Tampa, Florida. Three warehouses on the property were converted into large apartments, the TS offices, gym, and bunkrooms. There is also an obstacle course, a Main

Street shooting gallery, a helicopter pad, and more features necessary for training and missions.

In addition to the security business, there is a fourth warehouse that now houses an elite BDSM club, co-owned by Devon, Ian, and their cousin, Mitch Sawyer, who is the manager. A lot of time and money has gone into making The Covenant the most sought after membership in the Tampa/St. Petersburg area and beyond. Members are thoroughly vetted before being granted access to the elegant club.

There are currently over fifty Doms who have been appointed Dungeon Masters (DMs), and they rotate two or three shifts each throughout the month. At least four DMs are on duty at all times at various posts in the pit, playrooms, and the new garden, with an additional one roaming around. Their job is to ensure the safety of all the submissives in the club. They step in if a sub uses their safeword and the Dom in the scene doesn't hear or heed it, and make sure the equipment used in scenes isn't harming the subs.

The Covenant's security team takes care of everything else that isn't scene-related, and provides safety for all members and are essentially the bouncers. With the recent addition of the garden, and more private, themed rooms, the owners have expanded their self-imposed limit of 350 members. The fire marshal had approved them for 500 when the warehouse-turned-kink club first opened, but the cousins had intentionally kept that number down to maintain an elite status. Now with more room, they are increasing the membership to 500, still under the new maximum occupancy of 720.

Between Trident Security and The Covenant there's plenty of romance, suspense, and steamy encounters. Come meet the Sexy Six-Pack, their friends, family, and teammates.

∼

The Sexy Six-Pack (Alpha Team) and Their Significant Others

- Ian "Boss-man" Sawyer: Devon and Nick's brother; retired Navy SEAL; co-owner of Trident Security and The Covenant; husband/Dom of Angelina (Angel).
- Devon "Devil Dog" Sawyer: Ian and Nick's brother; retired Navy SEAL; co-owner of Trident Security and The Covenant; husband/Dom of Kristen; father of John Devon "JD."
- Ben "Boomer" Michaelson: retired Navy SEAL; explosives and ordnance specialist; husband/Dom of Katerina; son of Rick and Eileen.
- Jake "Reverend" Donovan: retired Navy SEAL; temporarily assigned to run the West Coast team; sniper; fiancé/Dom of Nick; brother of Mike; Whip Master at The Covenant.
- Brody "Egghead" Evans: retired Navy SEAL; computer specialist; husband/Dom of Fancy.
- Marco "Polo" DeAngelis: retired Navy SEAL; communications specialist and back up helicopter pilot; husband/Dom of Harper; father to Mara.
- Nick "Junior" Sawyer: Ian and Devon's brother; current Navy SEAL; fiancé/submissive of Jake.
- Kristen "Ninja-girl" Sawyer: author of romance/suspense novels; wife/submissive of Devon; mother of "JD."
- Angelina "Angie/Angel" Sawyer: graphic artist; wife/submissive of Ian.
- Katerina "Kat" Michaelson: dog trainer for law enforcement and private agencies; wife/submissive of Boomer.

- Millicent "Harper" DeAngelis: lawyer; wife/submissive of Marco; mother of Mara.
- Francine "Fancy" Maguire: baker; wife/submissive of Brody.

Extended Family, Friends, and Associates of the Sexy Six-Pack

- Mitch Sawyer: Cousin of Ian, Devon, and Nick; co-owner/manager of The Covenant, Dom to Tyler and Tori.
- T. Carter: US spy and assassin; works for covert agency Deimos; Dom of Jordyn.
- Jordyn Alvarez: US spy and assassin; member of covert agency Deimos; submissive of Carter.
- Tyler Ellis: Stockbroker; lifestyle switch—Dom to Tori; submissive to Mitch.
- Tori Freyja: K9 trainer for veterans in need of assistance/service dogs; submissive to Mitch and Tyler.
- Parker Christiansen: owner of New Horizons Construction; husband/Dom of Shelby; adoptive father of Franco and Victor.
- Shelby Christiansen: stay-at-home mom; two-time cancer survivor; wife/submissive of Parker; adoptive mother of Franco and Victor.
- Curt Bannerman: retired Navy SEAL; owner of Halo Customs, a motorcycle repair and detail shop; husband of Dana; stepfather of Ryan, Taylor, Justin, and Amanda. Lives in Iowa.
- Dana Prichard-Bannerman: teacher; widow of retired SEAL Eric Prichard; wife of Curt; mother of Ryan, Taylor, Justin, and Amanda. Lives in Iowa.

History of Trident Security & The Covenant

- Jenn "Baby-girl" Mullins: college student; goddaughter of Ian; "niece" of Devon, Brody, Jake, Boomer, and Marco; father was a Navy SEAL; parents murdered.
- Mike Donovan: owner of the Irish pub, Donovan's; brother of Jake; submissive/boyfriend of Charlotte.
- Charlotte "Mistress China" Roth: Parole officer; Domme/girlfriend of Mike; Whip Master at The Covenant.
- Travis "Tiny" Daultry: former professional football player; head of security at The Covenant and Trident compound; occasional bodyguard for TS.
- Doug "Bullseye" Henderson: retired Marine; head of the Personal Protection Division of TS.
- Rick and Eileen Michaelson: Boomer's parents; guardians of Alyssa. Rick is a retired Navy SEAL.
- Charles "Chuck" and Marie Sawyer: Ian, Devon, and Nick's parents. Charles is a self-made real estate billionaire. Marie is a plastic surgeon involved with Operation Smile.
- Dr. Roxanne London: pediatrician; Domme/wife (Mistress Roxy) of Kayla; Whip Master at Covenant.
- Kayla London: social worker; submissive/wife of Roxanne.
- Grayson and Remington Mann: twins; owners of Black Diamond Records; Doms/fiancés of Abigail; members of The Covenant.
- Abigail Turner: personal assistant at Black Diamond Records; submissive/fiancée of Gray and Remi.
- Chase Dixon: retired Marine Raider; owner of Blackhawk Security; associate of TS.

- Reggie Helm: lawyer for TS and The Covenant; Dom/husband of Colleen.
- Alyssa Wagner: teenager saved by Jake from an abusive father; lives with Rick and Eileen Michaelson.
- Carl Talbot: college professor; Dom and Whip Master at The Covenant.

The Omega Team and Their Significant Others

- Cain "Shades" Foster: retired Secret Service agent.
- Tristan "Duracell" McCabe: retired Army Special Forces
- Logan "Cowboy" Reese: retired Marine Special Forces; former prisoner of war. Boyfriend/Dom of Dakota.
- Valentino "Romeo" Mancini: retired Army Special Forces; former FBI Hostage Rescue Team (HRT) member.
- Darius "Batman" Knight: retired Navy SEAL.
- Kip "Skipper" Morrison: retired Army; former LAPD SWAT sniper.
- Lindsey "Costello" Abbott: retired Marine; sniper.
- Dakota Swift: Tampa PD undercover police officer; submissive girlfriend to Logan.

Trident Support Staff

- Colleen McKinley-Helm: office manager of TS; wife/submissive of Reggie.
- Tempest "Babs" Van Buren: retired Air Force helicopter pilot; TS mechanic.

- Russell Adams: retired Navy; assistant TS mechanic.
- Nathan Cook: former computer specialist with the National Security Agency (NSA).

Members of Law Enforcement

- Larry Keon: Assistant Director of the FBI.
- Frank Stonewall: Special Agent in Charge of the Tampa FBI.
- Calvin Watts: Leader of the FBI HRT in Tampa.
- Colt Parrish: Major Case Specialist, Behavioral Analysis Unit.

The K9s of Trident

- Beau: An orphaned Lab/Pit mix, rescued by Ian. Now a trained K9 who has more than earned his spot on the Alpha Team.
- Spanky: A rescued Bullmastiff with a heart of gold, owned by Parker and Shelby.
- Jagger: A rescued Rottweiler trained as an assistance/service animal for Russell.
- FUBAR: A Belgian Malinois who failed aggressive guard dog training. Adopted by Babs.
- BDSM: Bravo, Delta, Sierra, and Mike, two Belgian Malinoises and two German shepherds, the new guard dogs at the Trident compound that Ian named using the military communication's alphabet.

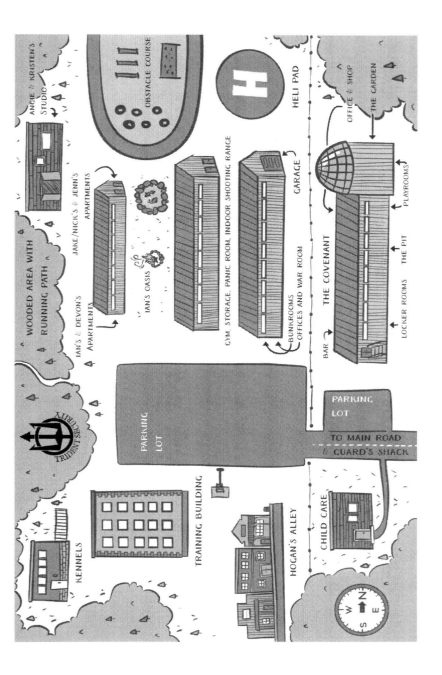

ONE

"Goddamn it!" Charlotte Roth slammed the landline phone down and stood from behind her desk laden with paperwork and folders. Sifting through three stacks of files, she found the one she needed. She then grabbed her cell phone, purse, and car keys before heading for the reception area of the Florida Department of Corrections, Tampa Probation and Parole office. Her holstered weapon and her DOC shield were attached to the belt of her pants. "I'm heading to booking. I'll be back later."

The department's receptionist, Julie Baxter, glanced up from her computer screen. "Which one got arrested?"

"Hector de la Cruz. Got caught up in a stolen property sting, the rat-bastard."

"You called it," Julie replied as she referenced her desk calendar. "And with three months to spare."

Over the years, Charlotte had gotten pretty good at guessing which of her ex-convicts would end up back in prison for violating the terms of their parole. De la Cruz had been an easy one, and even though she'd estimated he'd be screwing up within six months of his release, she was still a little surprised he'd done it so soon. His arrest just made her Monday morning even crappier.

She'd already been irritated when she woke up and remembered today was her thirty-fifth birthday—she hated birthdays. To top it off, a bunch of women she knew were throwing her a party tonight. She didn't mind the festivities as long as they were for someone else. But her friends had insisted on taking her out for food and drinks tonight, and in the end, it had been less of a hassle to accept than deal with their constant badgering. She'd even tried to thwart their plans by playing the Domme card, but it hadn't done much good outside of the club they all played in. She must be getting soft in her old age. Then again, she preferred dominating men, not women.

By the time she reached the Tampa PD's booking department on the other side of the city, she had a pounding headache. After parking in the monitored lot, she found the bottle of Tylenol she kept in the center console between the front seats and popped two in her mouth. She washed them down with water from a small bottle she kept in her purse.

Grabbing the file, she climbed out of her Chevy Tahoe and strode across the lot. The summer heat was returning, and by the time she reached the door, she was covered in a fine sheen of perspiration. Thankfully, they'd gotten the air conditioning fixed since the last time she'd been there because a cold blast cooled her down immediately as the door closed behind her, causing goose bumps to pebble over her skin.

The older police officer, sitting at the desk behind bulletproof glass, waved to her. "Hey, Charlotte, long time no see. How's my favorite parole officer?"

"I'm in a pissy mood and on my witch's broom today, Dan."

The man snorted, then grinned. "When aren't you? At least you didn't bring the flying monkeys with you. Who're you here for?"

"Hector de la Cruz. Detective Webb called me about a stolen property sting."

"Yeah, they brought in a bunch of them." He checked a piece of paper in front of him. "Let's see. Here he is—still in holding cell four, waiting to go for his arraignment." A buzzer sounded as he unlocked the door leading to the containment area for her. "Go on back."

"Thanks, Dan."

Having been there numerous times, she knew exactly where she was going. She found Isaac Webb and several other detectives in the area where they processed the paperwork for their arrests. Between them chatting with each other, radios squawking, prisoners complaining their rights had been violated—yeah, sure—and phones ringing, it wasn't surprising Webb didn't notice her until she dropped the file on the desk he was sitting at. His head snapped up. "Oh, hey, Charlotte. Thanks for coming so quickly. We're getting ready to run de la Cruz and a few others up to court. I'll put him at the top of the list so we can get you out of there as soon as possible."

She shook her head. "Thanks, Isaac, but that'll be impossible. Judge Hard-ass is on the bench today for arraignments."

The man's name was Phil Hardacre, but due to his courtroom demeanor, everyone called him by the moniker he'd earned, yet only when he wasn't within hearing distance. The bastard had no trouble throwing around the words "contempt of court," no matter which side of the law you were on.

The handsome Black man groaned and rolled his soft brown eyes. "Fuck." He glanced over his shoulder to where the other detectives were finishing their own paperwork. "Hey, Duggan, next time, check the damn court rotation before you schedule a sting, man. We'll be in court all afternoon with Hard-ass."

More groans and curses filled the room. One of the men crumpled up a piece of paper and wailed it at Duggan's head. He batted it away before it made contact. "Don't blame me. The lieutenant picked the date. I had nothing to do with it."

There were more groans and wads of paper thrown across the room. Ignoring everyone else, Charlotte turned back to Webb. "So, how'd you get roped into this detail?"

The man was a homicide detective, so having him take part in a property-crimes sting was a little out of the ordinary but not unheard of.

"Took it for an overtime shift. Marian's birthday is coming up in two months, and I want to surprise her with a trip to Hawaii. She's always wanted to go."

She grinned at the mention of his girlfriend of three years. "Any chance you're planning on making an honest woman out of her?"

Webb chuckled. "As a matter of fact, I already picked out the ring."

Her eyebrows shot up—she'd only been busting his chops. "Seriously?"

"Yup . . . with a kid on the way, the time's right."

"That's great, Isaac! Congratulations!"

A sappy grin spread across his face. "I love her two kids like they were my own, but they're both girls. I'm hoping this one will be a boy. But either way, it's gonna be awesome. I didn't have the whole infant bonding thing going on with the girls. They were five and six when Marian and I met. And let me tell you, they're over the moon that a new baby's on the way."

Pulling out his wallet, he showed her a recent picture of him, Marian, and the girls. "That's Crystal on the left and Reba on the right."

"They're adorable." A flash of something she couldn't quite identify swirled in her gut. She loved kids but didn't think she'd ever have one of her own. First off, she hadn't met anyone she was willing to have a long-term relationship with—it had to be someone willing to be topped—and even then, she was scared of bringing a child into this cruel world. It was impossible to watch a kid twenty-four hours a day and cushion them in bubble wrap so they never got hurt. Charlotte knew firsthand no one was ever really safe, even in their own home.

Handing him back the photo, she pushed the wayward thoughts from her mind. She steeled herself to spend the rest of the day in court, then put on a fake smile for her party later on. If the women who were taking her out weren't looking forward to a girl's night out without their significant others, she would've found a way to cancel. But the Domme in her couldn't disappoint them. Besides, after dealing with mostly dirtbags all day, she needed a distraction—an entertaining one at that.

"You really don't mind?"

Mike Donovan grinned at his employee, Jennifer Mullins. "Not at all, Baby-girl," he assured her, using the nickname her surrogate uncles had given her when she'd been an infant.

The six men who made up the original team at Trident Security had all served with Jenn's father on SEAL Team Four. When her parents had been murdered a few years ago, she'd come to live with her godfather, Ian Sawyer, one of the two brothers who owned the private security company.

"In this business, employees come and go. I always knew you'd be moving on to bigger and better things someday. In fact, I never quite understood why you came to work here in the first place. It's not like Ian's hurting for money."

Jenn was finishing up her third year of college, majoring in Social Work. She had the smarts and personality for a career helping others. "Grandpa Chuck and Grandma Marie always made sure their kids knew how to earn a living, and my parents had the same philosophy."

Chuck and Marie Sawyer were Mike's brother Jake's future in-laws, as he was engaged to their youngest son, Nick. Jake also worked for Nick's brothers, Ian and Devon, after serving in the Navy SEALs with them. Chuck was a self-made real estate billionaire, while his wife was a skilled plastic surgeon who often traveled to foreign countries with the organization Operation Smile. The couple considered Jenn their granddaughter. "Nothing worth having is handed to you on a silver platter, as Grandpa Chuck always says. I have a trust fund with the money from my parents' life insurance policies and the sale of the house in Virginia, but that's for my college tuition and maybe a house someday. And it wouldn't have felt right sponging off Uncle Ian—he's already done so much for me. Working here also took my mind off my parents' deaths when I first moved to Tampa. I love everyone that works at Donovan's, and it'll be hard to say goodbye, but I can't pass up the social work internship. I'll actually be in Kayla's office, so it'll be fun."

Kayla London and her wife, Roxy, were friends of the Sawyers and members of The Covenant, a BDSM club the brothers also owned. Jake was a club member, too, something Mike never quite understood. His younger sibling had gotten into the lifestyle in his teens. At first, Mike had thought it was a gay thing, but now he knew better. However, he still didn't get it. Gone were his thoughts that it harbored abusive behavior, but he couldn't figure out why

Jake and the others were—wired, he supposed the word was—differently. As long as no one was harmed, he guessed, then to each their own.

Mike leaned back in the desk chair in his small office at the back of the pub and smiled at Jenn as she stood in the doorway. "Well, we loved having you work here, and everyone will miss you too, but you better stop in as often as possible. Are you staying for Charlotte's birthday party after your shift?"

Jenn shook her head. "No, I've got a term paper due on Wednesday and another on Friday. Thanks again for everything, Mike. I'll help train whoever you get to replace me." She had given him three weeks' notice, so that was plenty of time to hire and train someone new.

A ding sounded in the kitchen, signaling an order up, and Jenn glanced over her shoulder. "That's probably mine."

"Go—I've got someone coming in to interview for Mario's position. Let me know when he gets here."

"Okay."

As she hurried toward the kitchen, Mike returned to the résumé in front of him. The night-time sous chef had up and quit without warning, so Mike was scrambling to fill the position before the weekend rolled around again. His daytime sous chef was covering both shifts for the overtime, but he wouldn't be able to do that for long.

The applicant coming in for the interview had been on a list of ex-felons who'd done their time and were looking for jobs. It was a local program to help them integrate back into society, and Mike had hired two other reformed felons to work in the kitchen in the past. One was still there after three years, while the other hadn't worked out, but after batting .500, Mike was willing to give someone else a shot.

Jose Perez had apparently been assigned to the prison

kitchen and learned a lot about food preparation during his two-year sentence for auto theft. From what the career organizer had told Mike, the guy had a fiancée and kid and had gotten involved with a chop-shop to provide for them. It was an all too common scenario for high school dropouts with no skills for work that was legal—they turned to a life of crime just to have a roof over their heads and food in their bellies. It could be a risk hiring an ex-con, but Mike firmly believed that most people deserved a second chance after they'd screwed up big time. He was a prime example.

Back when he was attending the local community college, his younger brother Jake had been the big man on campus at their high school. The starting quarterback for the football team and straight-A student, Jake had colleges throwing all sorts of incentives at him to get him to sign with them.

Meanwhile, Mike had been a B-student with no outstanding skills, who didn't excel in any sport, so he ended up being second best in his father's eyes. His destiny had been to eventually take over Donovan's Pub, the business his father and grandfather before him had owned. But a huge part of him had been extremely jealous of his younger brother back then.

A shelf above the bar had been filled with sports trophies Jake had won throughout his junior and senior high school years, in more than just football, and Mike had hated every single one of them. So when he'd accidentally found out seventeen-year-old Jake was gay, he did the worst thing he'd ever done in his life—he told their bigoted father.

At first, Sean Donovan had called his eldest son a liar, but then he'd stormed out of the house and headed for the adult video and toy store, where Mike had seen Jake kissing another guy before going inside. What Mike hadn't known at the time was in the basement of the store was an underground BDSM club. When Jake and his boyfriend, Max, had come back out two hours later, Sean followed Max home, where he'd beaten the living shit out of the guy, putting him in the hospital. The elder Donovan then returned home and tried to beat the gay out of his son.

That night had altered Jake's future in a way Mike had never expected, and he'd regretted telling the old man from the moment the words had come out of his mouth. After recovering from the assault, Jake graduated two months later, threw his full ride to Rutgers University in his father's face, and joined the Navy, all on the same afternoon.

The next day, all those trophies had disappeared from the shelf in Donovan's. Mike had found them in a box in the back of the pub's overcrowded store room years later after his father had died and he'd taken over the business.

Despite not knowing Mike had been responsible for their father finding out Jake was gay, the younger Donovan had distanced himself from his brother. Occasionally, he'd come home for the holidays, but mainly to see their mother. If he'd spoken more than a dozen words to their father for the rest of the old man's life, that would be a stretch.

When Jake moved back to Tampa with his teammates a few years ago, he and Mike began to see each other almost every week, but there was still a huge gap between them. Mike finally came clean to his brother when he realized what had happened all those years ago was negatively affecting Jake's relationship with Nick, thinking Jake would never want to speak to him again after his confession. As it turned out, instead of driving them further apart, it'd brought them closer together, a fact Mike would always be grateful for.

Shortly after, he'd pulled out the box of trophies and added them to a display case he'd put near the hostess stand, which was filled with the ones the pub's softball team had won over the past six years since he'd sponsored them.

A knock on the door had him glancing up to see Jenn

standing there again. "Your interview is here. I told him to have a seat in the party room. He seems like a nice guy—just a little nervous."

Mike stood and grinned. "Thanks, Ms. Social Worker."

She chuckled. "I like the sound of that."

Two

"Happy birthday, Mistress China," the women chorused while toasting her with their assorted alcoholic beverages.

Charlotte rolled her eyes and lifted her glass of wine. "Thank you, ladies. Now let's forget it's my birthday and pretend it's a girls' night out."

"Nope," Shelby Christiansen responded. "Not until you open your presents and cut the cake."

She pointed to the erotic confection that Fancy Evans had spent the day making at her bakery. She'd really done an amazing job, and Charlotte wondered if she'd used Brody's cock, abs, and hips as a model. She knew Fancy's husband/Dom was well-endowed, having seen him exposed at The Covenant, the elite BDSM club they both belonged to, on more than one occasion.

Despite not wanting a cake to begin with, Charlotte couldn't help but smirk. "It'll be a pleasure taking a knife to the guy's manhood. After all, I *am* a sadist." Well, not really, but she wouldn't tell any of the submissives that.

Laughter and hoots filled the private party room at the

back of Donovan's Pub. Mike Donovan's younger brother, Jake, was a Dominant and a Whip Master along with Charlotte at the club, but the two men didn't share the same need to be in the lifestyle.

"Open the presents first," Kristen Sawyer demanded with a giggle. Since having her baby a few months ago, the submissive had only had a few occasions to drink alcohol, so only a couple of sips into her second margarita, she was already giddy. In fact, the only ones not drinking any alcoholic beverages and feeling the effects were Kristen's sister-in-law, Angie Sawyer, and Fancy, who were both pregnant but still having a grand time. Thankfully, everyone else had arranged safe transportation for when the party was over.

Kayla London handed Charlotte a flat box that looked like it was from a clothing store, but knowing the exuberant submissive and her wife/Domme, Roxanne, it was doubtful it'd come from Macy's or Nordstrom's, whatever it was. "Open ours first!"

Glancing at Roxy, who was smirking, Charlotte shook her head. "This should be good." Ripping the paper from the box, she opened it and barked out a laugh. "Look out, subbies, Mistress China has a new whip!"

She pulled out the hot pink, braided leather whip and held it up for everyone to see. The women roared and cackled at the sight. "Is this the color I'm supposed to match when I'm beating someone's ass?"

"I bet Matthew will want you to use that on him!" Abigail Turner hooted. "You know pink is his favorite color."

Matthew was a gay submissive who was among the masochists at the club who liked to be serviced by one of the Whip Masters every week or two.

Charlotte continued to open the rest of the gifts. Some were funny gags, while others had been thoughtful and sentimental. By the time she was done, everyone was laughing and having a great time. It was fun to see them all in a different setting from the club occasionally, all letting their hair down and not having to follow protocol.

There were several Dommes at The Covenant, but Charlotte was only close to a few of them. She'd bonded with many of the submissives, however, finding herself being a bit of a mother hen toward them at times. It was part of her natural instincts which made her a Dominant in the lifestyle. She'd discovered the wonderful world of BDSM during her senior year in college, ironically through a guy she'd been dating who'd recognized her Domme qualities. They'd only been on their third date when he'd confessed he liked to be dominated by women in the bedroom.

At first, Charlotte had been shocked, but having an open mind, she listened to him describe the lifestyle and what he got out of it. Their next date had been to a local munch, where those interested in BDSM could meet with like-minded people and experienced Doms and subs. From the moment she'd walked into the place, she'd felt she'd found where she belonged.

While things had eventually ended between her and her first submissive, Charlotte had practiced the lifestyle ever since. She'd gone through every class offered in several clubs she'd belonged to and still took the occasional one to brush up on her skills. The last thing she'd ever want to do was inadvertently hurt a submissive—it would kill her if she did.

As the evening wore on, Charlotte relaxed more and could finally enjoy the fact she'd turned another year older. The conversations in the room were also growing louder and raunchier as the alcohol flowed. The sound of the women roaring with laughter drew the attention of a few people in the main bar. And, of course, a couple of swaggering jackasses had to poke their heads into the party room. Three barely-out-of-college-aged men strolled in after eyeballing the room full of women dressed to the nines.

Charlotte rolled her eyes. *Here it comes.*

"Hey, sexy ladies, mind if we join you?"

The laughter died down as Charlotte stood. In stocking feet, she was five-three, but in her four-inch heels, she at least came up to the shoulder of the brown-haired ogler who had spoken. "Actually, we do. This is a private party, so if you don't mind . . ."

The kid smirked. "Aw, don't be that way, sweetheart."

His dimples had a small smile spreading across her face, but then the jerk had to put his hand on her, running it up her bare arm. And that just pissed her off. One of the reasons she preferred the BDSM lifestyle was no one touched her without her permission.

She shoved his arm away and gave him her best Domme glare. "I'll be any way I want, jackass. Now, take your two friends and leave."

The kid had balls or a lack of brains. Either way, he reached out to touch her again. Charlotte was fully aware of how quiet the room had gotten, but she wasn't worried. Even though it was full of women, mostly submissives, none of them were shrinking violets. At least they weren't in her eyes. She sensed someone else stand behind her and knew instinctively it was the other Domme in the room, Roxanne London—pediatrician and a fellow Whip Master at The Covenant. While gentle with her patients, the tall, auburn-haired doctor was a force to be reckoned with when it came to protecting submissives.

Before the asshole could touch her again, Charlotte grabbed his wrist and twisted, shoving him against the wall, face first, with a thud. She lifted his hand behind his back until he went up on his toes and cried out in pain. His two buddies must have stepped forward to help him because a sudden *crack* split the air. Without looking, she knew Mistress Roxy had the new, pink bullwhip in her hand and had snapped a warning over their heads, freezing them in place.

"Uh-uh-uh, gentlemen. Stay right where you are. I missed on purpose—the next time, I won't."

Charlotte almost chuckled because she knew Roxy's wife, Kayla, loved when her Mistress went into full-protection mode and would be announcing she was horny as hell after this. But Charlotte had to deal with this asshole first. She hiked his arm a little higher, eliciting another yelp. "I tried to be nice, and you ignored my request, which was fine—you were trying to be cute. But then you had to put your paws on me without my permission, and that doesn't fly with me, little boy."

"What the hell?" The roared question had come from Mike Donovan as he strode in with two bouncers on his heels. "Charlotte, are you okay?"

With a final shove, she released the asshole, who spun around and growled at her. Due to her training, Charlotte immediately took a defensive stance, ready to kick the guy's ass. But before he could unleash his anger, Mike grabbed him by the arm and the back of his neck. "You're out of here."

He thrust the drunk toward the bouncers, then pointed at the two other intoxicated men. "You idiots are gone too. Don't let me see your faces until you learn to respect women. I don't tolerate this shit in my bar."

While the threesome was escorted out the door and through the main-room crowd, Mike turned to face the group of women. "Everyone, okay?"

Of course, it was Kayla who spoke first. "Yup! We didn't even need Ninja-girl to step in to help. Roxy and China took care of everything. Swoon! Damn, I'm horny now!"

The room filled with riotous laughter as the waitress

brought in another pitcher of margaritas. Ninja-girl was the nickname Kristen had earned during her first visit to The Covenant when she'd started dating one of the owners, Devon, who was now her husband. She'd interrupted two submissives bullying a third, Colleen Helm, in the locker room and had kicked their butts. Colleen had been grateful, and now that she was working for Trident Security as the office manager, she knew how to handle herself and was paying it forward whenever she saw someone being bullied.

Mike grinned at the group of women he'd gotten to know quite well over the past two years, then eyed Charlotte. "Gotta love a woman who kicks ass."

Crossing her arms, she stared at him with the commanding look she usually reserved for the submissives at the club and the men and women on probation with the law who had to check in with her every month. To her surprise, Mike's smile fell, and so did his gaze—not to her chest, hips, or legs like most men, but to her feet.

Well, hell. Who would have guessed? Master Jake's handsome older brother is a sexual submissive.

While Mike Donovan didn't have his brother's movie-star-worthy looks, he was still handsome in his own right. His hair was a lighter brown than Jake's, and instead of startling green eyes, his were hazel with a touch of amber. He stood six-foot even, five inches shorter than his younger brother, and although he wasn't as lean, his physique was toned enough to be admired.

Charlotte knew Jake and Mike hadn't been close for years, but that'd changed recently. They'd grown even closer over the past few months since Jake had moved back to Tampa. Apparently, Mike had taken his sibling up on an offer to work out at Trident's gym and training facilities with him. Charlotte hadn't realized until now that the slight beer belly the older Donovan brother used to sport was almost completely gone, and his arms, shoulders, and chest were leaner and more defined. All in all, a very tempting package, especially since he was exuding a submissiveness she hadn't noticed before now.

Was he aware of it? Well, that question was burning through Charlotte's mind at the moment, and she was looking forward to discovering the answer.

SITTING AT THE BAR, Mike sifted through the receipts, tallying up the credit charges for the evening. The cash was already in a deposit bag, which he'd drop into the slot of the TD Bank that was in the same shopping center as the pub. All of his employees had finished cleaning their work areas and restocked before leaving, and the only person left was one of the bartenders, Neil Patterson. And he was just about done putting everything away after the last stragglers had paid their tabs and left. The kitchen had been closed for over an hour, and most of the TVs and lights had been turned off.

Once he was certain he hadn't forgotten anything, Neil pulled his car keys out of his pocket and rounded the bar. "Need anything before I go?"

Mike shook his head. "Nope. How'd you do tonight?"

"Damn good. I think it was the best Monday night I've had this month."

The Irish pub was popular for both locals and tourists alike, and the tips for his employees were proof of that during the latter part of the work week and on the weekends, but Mondays tended to be the slowest of all the days. Tonight, however, had been much busier than usual. Even without Charlotte's birthday party in the back room, the waitresses and bar staff had been scurrying around, servicing the customers who'd run up quite a few hefty tabs.

"Glad to hear it. See you Thursday." The bartender had the next few nights off. "I'll shut off the lights and the rest of the TVs. Just lock the door on your way out. I'll be here for another twenty minutes or so."

"You got it."

Moments later, the front door closed, and Mike heard the lock engage. The ESPN recap of the night's baseball games was the only thing filling the air as he concentrated on logging everything into the books for his accountant. He wasn't sure what had suddenly made him aware he wasn't as alone as he'd thought—maybe it was the hair on the back of his neck standing up or the scent of light, sensual perfume over the usual bar odors—but whatever it was, it had him looking into the huge mirror behind the bar.

His heart thumped faster in his chest as his gaze met Charlotte's reflection. He'd been fantasizing about the woman for months now. Ever since he and Jake had gotten close, Mike had been getting to know his brother's friends better. He'd even been invited to parties at the Trident Security compound, and it was there he'd found himself drawn to the petite, Asian-American woman. Unfortunately, she was in the BDSM lifestyle, as was Jake and many of his friends, and Mike had no clue what it was really about and why they claimed to need it as badly as their next breath.

Her piercing, brown-eyed gaze pinned him in place. He swallowed hard as his dick twitched in his jeans. Her straight, black hair hung down past her shoulders, the tips of several strands curling against her collarbones, while subtle makeup highlighted her eyes, lips, and cheeks. The black knit shirt she wore had a deep V-neck that gave more than a hint of the inner swells of her breasts. Faded jeans that fit like a glove, a black belt, and black boots with four-inch heels completed her outfit. She was mouth-watering, and not for the first time since he'd met her, Mike wondered what it would be like to kiss her.

Charlotte took several sultry steps forward. "Your staff should be more diligent about checking the party room before turning out the lights."

"I'm sorry." Mike cleared his suddenly dry throat as it made his voice raspy and harsh. "I didn't realize you were still here, Charlotte."

Stopping behind him, she grabbed hold of the back of the bar stool he was sitting on and spun it around until he faced her. Even with her heels, he still had to look down at her. Never breaking eye contact, she used a single finger to make slow circles on his denim-covered thigh, just above his knee, and damn, if that didn't have his cock twitching some more. Her eyes bored into his again, and this time his gaze dropped. Since there was very little room between them, he was now focused on the skin exposed by her shirt's deep V.

"There's nothing to be sorry about, Michael. I stayed behind on purpose, wanting a few moments alone with you to see if I was right."

His brow narrowed as he tried to ignore her still swirling finger, even though he wanted to move it higher on his leg until she touched his groin. His gaze met hers again. "Right about what?"

"About your submissive nature when it comes to a dominant woman."

Annoyed at her presumption, Mike snorted. "I'm not some wimp who wants to be whipped by you, Charlotte."

He stood, forcing her to take a step backward, then moved to the side to put some more distance between them. It was the only way to get his throbbing cock under control. Having her stand so close that he could smell her enticing perfume was a recipe for disaster.

Crossing her arms, her eyes seemed to see straight into

his soul, and he fought the urge to swallow hard under her scrutiny. "I never thought you were a wimp, Michael. Is that what you think Nick is to Jake?"

Considering his soon-to-be brother-in-law had just retired from the Navy SEALs and joined his brothers' security company, the last thing he'd call Nick was a wimp. So why had Mike automatically thought that's what Charlotte saw in him? "No, I don't."

She stepped toward him, and Mike managed to stand his ground when what he really wanted to do was retreat. What was it about this woman that made his knees shake and his cock stand up and take notice?

Well, he knew the answer to the second part of that question—she was fucking gorgeous. It hadn't escaped his notice that every time she walked into the pub, practically every heterosexual male in the place eyed her up and down with lust-filled eyes. But anytime one of them approached her, they were shot down—nicely, for the most part. The only times he'd ever seen her annoyed was when any of them touched her without her consent—which is, apparently, what'd happened earlier with the drunken idiots.

She stood less than a foot away from him but didn't touch him. "Here's the deal, Michael. You know who I am . . . what I am. I'm a Domme who takes charge of her relationships, whether or not they involve sex. Most of them don't."

She shrugged unapologetically. "I'm selective when it comes to sex. That doesn't mean I can't offer submissives the domination they crave. However, if there's a man I'm interested in—one who's sexually submissive—I have no qualms about approaching him. I've always thought you were attractive, but until earlier tonight, I thought you were off limits to me—I wasn't aware of your submissiveness."

When he opened his mouth to contradict her, she held up a hand to silence him. "Don't deny it. When I assert myself, you immediately drop your gaze to the floor. I can see right now you're doing your best not to put more distance between us, and it's not because you're not attracted to me. That bulge in your jeans tells me otherwise.

"Now, I know this has caught you off guard. You'll need time to think about it, and that's fine. But just to make myself clear, and so there's no confusion on your part, I'm offering you a chance to explore your submissiveness, preferably with sex involved, and to learn all about the power exchange the BDSM lifestyle is based on."

She reached over and grabbed a bar napkin and the pen he'd been using. "Safety is very important to me, and this is not something to jump into without properly researching it—in fact, it's imperative. This will be unlike any relationship you've ever had before, and I can almost guarantee it will be the best one you've ever had. These are two websites I want you to go to and research the lifestyle. Go to the chat rooms and ask questions. Then, when you're ready to give me your answer, here's my cell phone number. Call me next Monday, no sooner, no later, and let me know your decision."

Handing him the napkin with the information on it, she smiled provocatively. "I hope the answer is yes. Have a good night, Michael."

Mike's jaw almost hit the floor when the seductress turned and strode to the front door, unlocked it, and left without a backward glance. He swallowed the lump that had been in his throat as she'd told him what she wanted from him. His cock pulsated, and it took every ounce of self-control not to run after her and ask what it would take to end up in her bed tonight.

Silence filled the air as seconds ticked by. Running a hand down his face, Mike shifted his hips. "Holy shit."

Three

As he poured a glass of draft beer for one of his midday regulars, Mike glanced up when the front door to Donovan's swung open. His gut churned, and he tried to act as if nothing was wrong as Nick strode into the bar, drawing many appreciative looks from the women around the room, young and old. The youngest Sawyer brother was six feet tall and about two-hundred pounds of pure muscle. Like his siblings, his hair was jet black, which offset his startling blue eyes. Even though Mike was straight, it was easy to see how Jake had fallen for the good-looking guy.

Since Mike had called Nick and asked him to stop by for a chat—without Jake—it wasn't a surprise he was here. But as he took a stool at the bar, Mike was starting to regret calling him in the first place. He tried to act natural as he gave old man Jeffers his beer. "Hey, Nick. What'll you have?"

"Bud Light is fine. What's on the specials today? I'm starved."

Mike snorted as he grabbed a beer bottle from the cooler and a daily menu—the guy knew the regular menu by heart.

"What? Doesn't Jake feed you? You're always starving when you come in here."

"Actually, he had to fly up to D.C. with Ian yesterday for some meeting about one of TS West's contracts." Jake had spent a year and a half out in California getting the West Coast team set up, while Nick had been finishing up his last tour with the Navy before retiring and joining his brothers in Tampa. From what Mike had figured out from conversations he'd heard when visiting the Trident compound, that meeting was, most likely, someplace inside the Pentagon. "They won't be back until tomorrow, so I'm on my own."

Scanning the menu, he chose the daily burger special, then took a swig of his beer as Mike entered the order into the computer behind the bar. When he turned back around, Nick eyed him curiously. "So . . . what did you need to talk about—without Jake?"

Mike glanced up and down the bar. "Um . . . not here." He raised his voice. "Hey, Missy, I'll be in the party room if you need me."

The daytime bartender waved at him as she took an order from one of the waitresses. Grabbing a beer for himself from the cooler, he cocked his head toward the room on the other side of the restaurant and said to Nick, "Let's go in there."

The younger man followed and then sat across from him at a table at the back of the party room. Throughout the week, it didn't get much use, but during lunch and dinner on the weekends, the overflow from the dining room ended up in there unless there was a scheduled event.

Unsure of how to start the conversation, Mike asked, "So . . . how are you doing?"

Nick arched an eyebrow at him. "That's what you wanted to talk about? Let's skip the bullshit—what's bugging you?"

Taking a deep breath, Mike let it out slowly. He couldn't look Nick in the eye. Instead, his gaze was on the beer bottle label he was picking at with his fingernail. "How . . . how did . . ." He swallowed hard. "How did you know you were . . . um . . ."

"Spit it out, Mike. How did I know I was gay?"

He shook his head. "No . . . not that . . . um . . . how did you know you were a submissive?"

Silence filled the air. Seconds passed by until Mike finally couldn't take the suspense anymore and raised his chin. He didn't expect to see Nick's mouth opening and closing while surprise and bewilderment filled his eyes.

Finally, Nick gave his head a shake and ran a hand through his short hair. "Sorry, Mike. That's got to be the last question I ever expected to hear from you. Give me a minute to switch gears here." He took a swig of his beer. "Okay, how did I know? Um, I didn't . . . not until Jake and I hooked up after Dev and Kristen's wedding. Jake did his Dom thing, and I don't know—it just felt right. Trust me, I was confused as all hell. I'd never been in a relationship like that before—or even had a one-night stand like that. It was definitely different, but like I said, it felt right. Why are you asking?"

He should have known that question was coming, but it still took him a moment before he could admit to Nick and himself what had been going through his mind for the past three days. "I . . . ah . . . shit, how do I say this? Charlotte was here the other night . . . after closing . . . and . . . uh . . . she came onto me . . . I guess—"

"Wait—what do you mean she came onto you? Charlotte doesn't date outside the lifestyle, as far as I know."

"She offered to introduce me to it . . . she wants me to submit to her."

"Charlotte?" Nick's eyebrows were almost up to his hairline. "*Mistress China* made an appearance and offered to . . . um . . . okay . . . wow. Okay, so I guess my next question is . . .

how do you feel about that? Obviously, you've given it some thought since we're discussing it."

Mike shrugged. "Yeah, I'm attracted to her—I'd have to be dead or gay not to be—but I . . . I don't know about this getting on my knees shit—"

His words were cut off when Nick threw his head back and barked out a laugh. "Ha! Oh, shit . . . this is too funny . . . wait . . . give . . . give me a minute here."

Nick's cheeks turned red as his shoulders shook. It took a few moments for him to get himself under control. At first, Mike was annoyed, but then he couldn't help the grin that spread across his face. "All right, jackass . . . knock it off and help a guy out—I'm out of my element here."

"Oh, shit . . ." He wiped his eyes and took a deep breath. "Okay . . . okay, sorry. Um . . . all right. Well, I've gotten to know Charlotte over the past few months—despite being a bit of a sadist, she's really cool. I know you've figured out that the lifestyle isn't a bad thing, but I get the impression you still don't realize it's a good thing for many people."

When Mike nodded, Nick continued. "Jake and I were at a munch at the club we belonged to in San Diego—a munch is a get-together for newbies or people interested in the lifestyle to meet and talk to experienced subs and Doms. There's no play, just questions and answers. One of the male subs there gave a great explanation of the lifestyle. He compared it to the military—which, being in San Diego, helped a lot of people get it.

"In the military, there are two types of people—officers and the rank and file. Officers, obviously, issue the commands—they're the leaders or Dominants. Rank and file are the followers, a.k.a. submissives. One without the other means nothing works—the dynamics of the squad won't work unless both parties perform their roles and duties. No matter what, there are those who won't be able to function without that leader—they know how to follow orders, but when it comes to planning a mission, they're lost. For the leaders, if there's no one to follow their orders, then they'll lose the battle. Can't lead if no one follows.

"The same goes for a D/s relationship—it won't work unless the Dom and sub have mutually agreed upon roles that they stick to. Doms take the lead, ensuring their subs are taken care of, and do everything they can to make sure their subs are protected. In return, the subs agree to hand over the responsibility of play and other aspects of their lives to their Doms. For those not in the lifestyle, it might seem that the Doms have all the control, but in reality, the subs have the ultimate power through their limit lists and safewords, and those need to be respected at all costs.

"The same goes for the military—if there's no respect and trust, the subordinates aren't going to follow the leaders. They'll do the minimum required to avoid being put on report or court marshaled, but the moment the shit hits the fan, they'll turn tail and run. It's not cowardice but self-preservation. Most rank and file will never be leaders. Most subs will never be Doms. They can try, but I guarantee, once they can put their lives in someone else's hands again—someone they trust—they're relieved."

Nick paused and sipped his beer as the daytime waitress brought his lunch in. "Need anything else, Nick?" she asked, placing the plate piled high with the burger special and fries and a ketchup bottle in front of him.

"Nope. Thanks, Joanie." When she left the room again, Nick picked up a french fry, popped it into his mouth, and grabbed the ketchup bottle. "Does any of that make sense to you, or did I make you more confused?"

Mike let everything his future brother-in-law said sink into his brain before taking a deep breath and letting it out slowly. "No, I think you gave me another way of looking at it." He snorted. "I was so caught off guard, I told Charlotte I didn't want to be her wimp."

Pausing with his burger an inch or two from his mouth, Nick's eyes widened. "Damn, I wish I'd been a fly on the bar for that. What'd she say?"

"She asked if I thought you were a wimp for submitting to Jake." He quickly held up a hand, not wanting the younger man to think he was putting him down. "I don't—that's the last word I'd ever use to describe you or Jake. But it's different between you and him."

Nick chewed the bite he'd taken, then swallowed. "What, because we're both men, and Charlotte's a woman, and you don't think men should submit to women?"

"Yeah . . . no . . . I don't know." He ran a hand down his face. The frustration was killing him. He hadn't dated in a while, but there'd been a few one-night stands—a perk, of sorts, of owning a bar. But those were getting fewer and further apart. He was at the point in his life where quick hookups with nameless women weren't doing much for him anymore. Yeah, the release with someone was better than what he got with his hand, but meaningless sex was starting to grate on him.

His buddies had all settled down over the past ten years—it had worked for some but not all of them, so there were a few divorces. Mike didn't want to marry someone just for the sake of getting married. He wanted what his brother and Jake's coworkers and friends had all found. Someone to grow old with—someone they'd found the other half of their heart and soul in.

He wished his soulmate would just walk through the door of the pub one day and announce she was the one he'd been looking for. But that shit only happened in fairy tales. So that meant he had to start dating again . . . getting himself out there, meeting women he was attracted to . . . women like Charlotte . . . no, not Charlotte. *Well, why not?*

"Why not, what?"

Nick's question brought Mike back to the here and now, not realizing he'd spoken aloud. "Should I . . . should I try this Dominant/submissive thing with her? I mean, I am attracted to her . . . big time. I just never thought she was interested in me. We've had some casual conversations before, and everything was fine. But, honestly, now, I'm a little intimidated. It's like suddenly she's set her sights on me, and my knees are shaking. And don't even get me started on the whole whip thing. I know you and Jake have both done that, but there's no way I could stand there and take someone whipping me."

Grabbing a paper napkin, Nick pointed to the pen Mike had forgotten was behind his ear. "Let me have the pen. There are a few sites for you to check out and where you can talk to other subs—men and women, gay and straight."

He jotted down several websites, two of which Charlotte had already told Mike to visit, before handing back the pen and the napkin. "The one thing I do know is Charlotte has had D/s relationships before that didn't include the whip—I'm not sure how long they lasted, but I remember Jake mentioning it at some point. It's not for everyone. Why she got into it is something you'll have to ask her—I have no idea. But that's the great thing about the lifestyle. You sit down and negotiate what your contract involves—you list what your hard and soft limits are—what you're okay with, and what turns you off. Then the Dom and sub come to an agreement, and it's solid. Unless, of course, you're dealing with a wannabe who's in the lifestyle for the wrong reasons."

He popped another fry into his mouth, chewed, and then swallowed it before continuing. "You know, one of the things I love about our D/s relationship is there's no guessing what

Jake's thinking. If something is bothering one of us, we sit down and hash it out—that's something I never did in a relationship before, and I think that's what makes this one so special. I trust Jake more than any other man I've ever dated. I know if I'm having a bad day, I can go home and count on him to help me get past it. There's something about shutting my mind down and just letting him take over that . . . I don't know how to say it for you to really understand, but I guess the best way to put it is it sets me free and grounds me at the same time. I can't really explain it any other way. All I know is that if I had to choose right here and now between having a D/s relationship with Jake or having a vanilla world relationship, it would be no contest. Once you go Dom . . ." He shook his head and grinned. ". . . all right, that won't rhyme, but you get the point."

Yeah, Mike got the point—the problem was he still wasn't sure if he was out of his mind for even considering taking Charlotte up on her offer.

STRIPPED down to his boxer briefs, straddling Jake's ass on their bed, Nick kneaded the hard flesh of his lover's naked back. As soon as Jake had gotten home from his D.C. trip, Nick had asked his Dom to indulge him. It was one of the things he enjoyed doing, giving Jake a massage, mainly because of the scars that marred his skin. Most of the time, it led to sex, but sometimes it ended with cuddling.

It had been a huge turning point in their relationship when Jake had finally stopped hiding the damage his father's belt had done all those years ago. It confirmed there were no more secrets between them, which was why Nick knew he had to spill his guts. He just hoped the massage would relax Jake enough so he wouldn't flip out. "So, everything went okay at the Pentagon?"

"Mmm-hmm," Jake mumbled into his pillow. "Damn, that feels good, babe. Keep it up, and we'll never make it to the club later."

After leaving Donovan's, Nick knew he had to tell Jake about his conversation with Mike. Thank God his future brother-in-law hadn't sworn him to secrecy. Nick wasn't sure if Mike had forgotten to tell him not to inform Jake or if he'd just assumed Nick would keep his mouth shut. Knowing something that concerned Jake's brother and not telling him about it was one sure way for Nick to earn a punishment, and not one that would result in any pleasure afterward. Lying by omission was just as bad as outright lying in Jake's book. He was protective of his family and friends—his role as a Dom just reinforced that.

"Mmm. So what did you do while I was gone? Mom mentioned you stopped by this morning when I spoke to her on my way home."

Nick slid his hands downward and found another knot of muscles. He dug the heel of his palm in, trying to loosen it. "I just swung by to see if she needed anything and ended up cleaning out expired food from her refrigerator and cabinets, taking out the trash, changing a dead light bulb in the hallway, and helping her pay some bills." He paused. "I think it's time to have that talk with her and Mike about her going into the assisted living facility."

They'd noticed recently that Emma Donovan was slowing down and needed more help doing many things she used to do without a problem. They were worried about her driving too and tried to keep track of her shopping needs and appointments so they could take her. "She's getting worse, Jake. I think you should call her doctor again—tell him it looks like she'll need the testing after all."

Mrs. Donovan's father had briefly suffered the start of Alzheimer's when he'd wandered out into traffic and gotten hit by a car twenty-six years ago. While it'd been hard on the family, in a way, it'd been a blessing they hadn't had to watch him go downhill as the unforgiving disease took over his brain for good. For the past few months, her sons and Nick had started to notice signs she might also have developed the disease, but she hadn't wanted to undergo the testing her doctor had suggested. It was probably due to her fear of the unknown and wishing denial would prevent it from worsening. Nick hoped like hell it didn't happen to every generation on Jake's maternal side of the family.

"Yeah. I think that's a good idea—hopefully, she'll agree this time. I was going to go talk to Mike about it tomorrow anyway."

Nick cleared his throat. Now was as good a time as any. "Yeah, about Mike . . . I . . . um . . . had lunch with him yesterday."

At the hesitancy, Jake picked up his head and glanced over his shoulder. "What's wrong?"

"Nothing . . . not really . . . I mean . . . it could be a good thing . . . I think . . . but I don't know if—"

In one swift move, Jake flipped over, sending Nick onto his back on the other side of the bed, cutting off the last of whatever he'd been about to say. Before the younger man could react, his Dom was on top of him, his hands on Nick's wrists, pinning them to the mattress.

Annoyance, combined with concern, flared in Jake's eyes. "Spit it out, Junior. What's going on with Mike?"

Shit. Should have waited until after we had sex.

With a heavy sigh, Nick tried to ignore Jake's semi-hard cock touching his fully-erect one through two layers of thin cotton briefs. "He called and asked me to stop by for lunch and talk privately. He . . . um . . . had some questions . . . about the lifestyle . . . about being a submissive."

Jake's eyes narrowed. "Why would Mike have questions

about being a sub? We never hid our D/s relationship around him—not since you were in the hospital."

Early in their relationship, Nick had gotten shot while trying to save a teenage girl from her perverted father. During his recovery, Mike visited him and Jake and confessed his role in Sean Donovan finding out his youngest son was gay.

"Apparently, he and Charlotte had a . . . conversation, I guess . . . actually, it was more like Mike and Mistress China had a conversation . . . when she told him he was submissive and offered—"

Jake's grip on Nick's wrists tightened, and a fierce scowl spread across his face. "What! Are you telling me Charlotte offered to introduce my brother—my *vanilla* brother—to the lifestyle?"

"Um . . . yeah. But I don't—"

His words were cut off again as Jake cursed and released him before jumping off the bed and reaching for his discarded jeans. "Is she fucking nuts? What the hell was she thinking?"

Nick sat up. "Jake, I don't think—"

"I'm going to talk to her—she's at the club, teaching a class right now." He pulled his T-shirt back on, then shoved his bare feet into a pair of sneakers. "I'll be back later."

"Jake—hey, Jake!"

The Dom paused in the doorway and glanced back. When he saw the "what the fuck?" expression on Nick's face, he strode back into the room. Leaning down and grabbing the back of Nick's neck, he pulled him close and slammed their lips together. It was a hard and fury-filled kiss as Jake plunged his tongue into Nick's mouth, exerting his dominance. But it didn't last long.

Releasing his sub, Jake straightened. "I'm sorry, babe. I'll make it up to you tonight, but I have to go talk to Charlotte and find out what the hell is going through her mind."

Realizing Jake wouldn't let this go without confronting the Domme, Nick nodded. "Okay. Do you want me to meet you there in a bit, or are you coming back here?"

They'd made plans to go out to dinner and the movies, followed by a visit to The Covenant. A full date night was something they didn't often find time for with their schedules, and Nick had been looking forward to it all day.

"Wait here. I'll come back and change, then we'll go grab dinner before the movie." Pivoting, he headed for the doorway but paused at the threshold and glanced back. "And, Junior, you earned an extra-long blowjob later for telling me. Thank you."

Nick grinned as his Dom disappeared into the hallway. Sometimes there were definitely advantages to spilling the beans.

Four

"How long does subspace last after intense play?"

With her arms crossed over her chest, Charlotte paced back and forth in front of the class she and Master Stefan Lundquist were giving in the garden on the second floor of The Covenant. Shrubbery, trees, flowers, and artificial grass in between all the play areas combined to make it look like the Garden of Eden. It was part of the new addition to the building and had a retractable roof for when the weather was nice—they'd probably be opening it tonight as the temperatures outside cooled.

The club's manager, Mitch Sawyer, who co-owned the business with his cousins, Ian and Devon, had gotten together with the managers and owners of other clubs in the area to set up a schedule of classes to educate Doms and submissives in different types of bondage, suspension, and impact play. Rotating through the clubs twice a month, a different topic was taught.

This evening, she and the Coast Guard lieutenant— whoops, lieutenant commander, as he'd just been promoted —had gone over the sub-categories of each type of play, the basics, safety, and ultimate goals—what the couples hoped to achieve. The participants were all relatively new to the lifestyle and were still exploring which varieties of play they were interested in. Stefan's contracted submissive, Cassandra —one of the club's waitresses—was also present for demonstration purposes.

"Good question," Charlotte responded, stopping in front of the man who'd asked it. Although he was new to the lifestyle, she could see Master Wayne Gifford had the potential to be a good Dom. He was very attentive to Nancy Walker, the submissive woman sitting on a pillow beside his chair. He took every advantage to touch her and make sure she was comfortable. The looks the sub occasionally gave him said she felt safe with him.

However, his blond-haired buddy, Master Roy Carpenter, was a completely different story. He'd been pretty much ignoring his sub, Susan, and appeared too much into the pain aspects of the play and not the resulting pleasure. In fact, he'd been leering at Charlotte since the class had started. She knew most men found her attractive, but it took much more than just their interest in her body for her to return that interest.

She was dressed in her usual club wear since tonight was her turn in the Whip Master rotation. The black, sleeveless catsuit clung to her every curve, and her over-the-knee, black leather boots only added two inches to her height. She found them more comfortable when she was going to be standing for a few hours.

Unfortunately, the asshole Dom-wannabe had been eyeing her as if her outfit was an invitation for him to hit on her. Charlotte would have to tell Mitch not to allow him to sign up for another class—he was here for all the wrong reasons. His sub, though, would be better off without him.

Charlotte would have to see if she could get the woman alone at some point and find out if she could help her.

Susan Kelly was definitely a submissive, but with the wrong Dom, she could be seriously harmed—physically, mentally, or emotionally—and that was the one thing Charlotte refused to stand by and watch. She had no problem interfering with another Dominant and their submissive if it was warranted. The Covenant's owners, Masters Ian, Mitch, and Devon, had no problem with it either. That was one of the many reasons Charlotte played in this club only and not any of the other clubs throughout the area—submissives were protected at all costs.

"There are several things that factor into how long it lasts. Genetics and body makeup, pain threshold, time of day, activities the sub engaged in before the play, and how intense the play was. Is the sub on any prescription or recreational drugs, and how do they affect her? Is alcohol involved? You all know how much we stress that participants should not drink alcohol before intense play. And it should be limited before mild play. Consumption is closely monitored here at The Covenant, but most clubs don't have the resources, so it's up to the Dom to ensure that rule is followed."

She referenced her mental checklist, knowing there were a few more things she needed to mention. "The environment also factors in—some subs will be more relaxed at home or in a private playroom than out on the club floor. What's the sub's state of mind going into the play—were they having a stressful day? Are you celebrating a birthday, anniversary, or collaring ceremony? Are there things on their mind that are preventing them from totally giving in to the play? Things like that.

"The best answer I can give for how long it will last for an individual sub is I don't know. There's no right or wrong answer to that—it's very subjective to the sub's response to the stimuli. In most cases, experienced subs can tolerate more pain, and as a result, that can prolong subspace. It's the Dom's responsibility to pay attention to the cues displayed by the sub's speech and body language. You must become attuned to your sub's responses and learn from experience. When in doubt, err on the side of caution."

The Dom smiled and nodded, clearly satisfied with her explanation. Charlotte stepped back and eyed the rest of the class. "Any other questions?"

A Domme in her mid-fifties, with a younger male submissive at her feet, spoke up next. "How will I know when it's safe to leave my sub alone for a few minutes as he comes down from subspace after an intense scene?"

"Ask him a few simple questions—does he know where he is, what the date is, what's four times eight—stuff like that, and see how quickly and accurately he answers. Ask how he's feeling—is he dizzy, tired, or sore? Can he keep his eyes open? Can he visually track a finger moving back and forth in front of his face? If he's still a little foggy and slow, then stay with him and ask some more questions in a few minutes. I've seen subs take several hours to completely recover after an intense scene, while others are back to normal within twenty or thirty minutes.

"Make sure your sub drinks plenty of water as he comes down from subspace—you don't want him to get dehydrated. As a rule of thumb, keep an eye on him for a full two hours after the scene has ended. Aftercare, as you've all been told, is the most important part of a scene." She paused, then asked again, "Any other questions?"

"Mistress China, may I have a word with you, please . . . alone?"

Charlotte turned around slowly at Jake's low voice and the barely-controlled anger in it. She hadn't heard or seen him enter the garden—like the rest of his military-trained teammates, he tended to walk on silent feet.

Beside her, Stefan raised a curious eyebrow at the other Dom but didn't interfere. Instead, he clapped his hands and gestured toward a play area to his right. "All right, class. Let's finish up tonight's lesson with a brief Shibari demonstration—we have about thirty minutes before the staff arrives to get the club ready to open so I can show you a simple example. Cassandra, please remove your bra and present for me."

Jake was ignoring everyone else in the garden. His heated glare told Charlotte all she needed to know. He'd found out about her proposition to Mike and was pissed. If she'd been a submissive, she'd be quaking in her boots at his hard expression and tight jawline, but she knew him well enough to know she wasn't in any danger. Master Jake would never raise a hand to a woman unless it were in self-defense.

With him being six feet five and two-hundred-ten pounds of solid, alpha-male muscle, she doubted many women on Earth would try to take him on for one reason or another. If there were, they were probably followers of al Qaeda or ISIS and lived on the other side of the world.

Keeping her expression neutral, she nodded once. "Certainly, Master Jake. We can talk in one of the playrooms."

Pivoting on the balls of her feet, she strode toward a staircase that led to the pit and two dozen playrooms, knowing full well he was on her heels even though his footsteps didn't make a sound. It didn't matter which room they used since they weren't there for play. At the bottom of the stairs, Charlotte opened the first door to her left and entered the one with a "Major League Baseball Locker Room" theme. As Jake shut the door behind him, she hopped up onto a padded physical therapy table, crossed her arms and legs, and pasted a well-practiced expression of indifference on her face.

Leaning against one of the metal lockers that stored play

equipment, the Dom also crossed his arms and glared at her. "Something you want to tell me, Charlotte?"

She swung her foot back and forth. "Something that's none of your business? No, there isn't, Jake."

He growled. "Enough with the games, damn it. You know what I'm talking about. Mike doesn't belong in this lifestyle."

"I beg to differ. Since I'm almost positive he didn't go to you with any questions he had, that only leaves Nick, who knows better than to keep a secret from his Dom. The fact that Mike spoke to Nick at all tells me my offer to help him explore the lifestyle made an impression on him."

Jake pushed off the locker and stalked the room's width, back and forth, his frustration climbing. "That doesn't mean it's for him. I don't want him getting screwed up in the head just because he's got a hard-on for you."

If anyone else had said that to her, Charlotte's claws would have come out. But their friendship was deep enough for her not to take offense, knowing Jake was just being his normal protective self when it came to his loved ones. She knew part of his reaction had to do with his bastard of a father and how the man had favored Jake, a star on his high school football team, over his firstborn, Mike. That favoritism had caused a chasm between the two siblings that had only recently been closed again.

Charlotte cocked her head to the side. "Jake, how long have you known me?"

Stopping short, he put his hands on his hips. "I don't know—four or five years."

"And in that time, have you ever known me to harm a submissive—emotionally, mentally, or physically?" There was a huge difference between inflicting pain for pleasure and harming a sub, and Jake would know full well what she was referring to.

Seconds ticked by before Jake let out an exasperated

breath. "No, you'd never harm a submissive—I know that. And shit, I know I'm the last person that should be questioning you. Nick didn't know squat about the lifestyle, and Dev and Ian gave me the same crap when they found out."

He ran a hand down his face, then shook his head. "I'm sorry. You were right earlier—it's none of my business."

Sliding off of the table, Charlotte stepped over to him. "I never would've approached him if I didn't see him respond to me in a submissive manner. I won't hurt him, Jake. There will be a contract in place *if* he wants to explore."

She made sure his gaze was on hers as she added, "This is the last time you and I will have this discussion. He's a big boy and doesn't need his brother running interference for him."

After a moment, Jake nodded. "Understood."

"Good." Charlotte grinned. "And don't worry. I promise I won't have him showing off his junk when you're around."

Jake snorted and rolled his eyes. "For that, I thank you." He held his arms out. "Forgive me for being an ass?"

Stepping into his embrace, she hugged him back. "Of course. Good friends are hard to come by."

PICKING up his cell phone from the bar, Mike entered the number written on the napkin but stopped just shy of hitting the send button, just like he'd done the other five times he'd tried to call Charlotte in the past hour. He had an interview for the waitress position in thirty minutes and not much else to do in between. The ex-con he'd hired the other day seemed to be working out so far, and as usual, the rest of his staff was handling the slow Monday afternoon crowd without any help from him.

He hadn't seen or heard from Charlotte since the night of

her birthday party and couldn't get her out of his mind. Had she told him to call earlier than today, his answer to her proposed relationship would probably have been no. But with the extra time, he found himself thinking about her nonstop and what she wanted from him—what she'd offered him.

After reading about all the different topics concerning BDSM on the websites she'd given him, he'd gotten more confused. Not about the basics of the lifestyle—those were pretty easy to understand—but the fact that he was being drawn toward something he'd never been interested in before. Then, after talking to Nick, Mike returned to the sites and started asking questions in the chat rooms using a random sign-in name he'd pulled out of thin air. He'd been surprised at the number of male submissives who were in careers that were considered to be alpha-male oriented—firemen, police officers, an MMA fighter, a bull rider, and plenty of others—that is if they'd been telling the truth behind the anonymous shroud of the internet.

The hardest part had been when he and Jake had been at the Trident Security gym the day after Mike had spoken to Nick. At first, while doing different exercises with free weights, they'd talked about their mother and how to get her to consent to the dementia testing and to consider selling the home she'd lived in for forty years. Whether she was in the early stages of Alzheimer's or not, with her advancing age and declining ability to take care of herself, the best thing was to move her into an assisted living facility where the staff could keep a closer eye on her. Her medications would be administered on time, something they suspected she wasn't doing at the moment, and the staff would help her shower and do her laundry. Her meals would also be monitored, and the staff would check on her during the day and night to make sure she hadn't fallen.

Both Jake and Mike worked wacky hours, and there were times Jake had to leave town with almost no notice for a mission or case. Running a restaurant required Mike to work odd hours and be on call when he was off in case a situation arose his staff couldn't handle. The siblings could hire someone to care for their mother in her home, but with an assisted living facility, there'd be more people her age around and activities other than watching mindless TV all day.

Once that part of their conversation was over, and Mike had switched to the bench press, Jake had started with, "So . . . I heard you and Nick had a conversation the other day."

With the weighted bar fully extended over his head, Mike froze and narrowed his eyes at his brother spotting behind him in case his muscles gave out toward the end of the set of repetitions. He couldn't be mad at Nick for blabbing to Jake because Mike couldn't honestly remember if he'd asked him not to. Either way, it was clearly out in the open. Slowly controlling the bar's descent toward his upper chest, Mike tried to make his response sound indifferent. "Yeah. Figured out of everyone I knew, he'd be the best person to talk to about . . . it." That was the only word that came to mind—he didn't know what "it" was exactly, but the word encompassed everything running through his mind. "No offense."

"None taken. And I agree—Nick can describe the flip side of things better than I could. It's been a long time since I was on the submissive side of the lifestyle." He paused. "So, did you come to a decision yet? Charlotte's a good Domme to learn from."

Mike came just short of locking his elbows with the bar held high. "Huh. I thought you'd be against her and me."

Jake watched the weights go down again, waiting for the moment he'd have to reach out and assist with a lift. "At first, I was —I even went to ream her a new one before she, rightfully, put me in my place."

43

When Mike faltered, and his gaze slammed into Jake's, his brother made sure he wouldn't drop the weight before holding up a hand. "I promise I won't interfere again. She'll kick my ass if I do." He shrugged his sculpted shoulders. "I guess I always just assumed it wouldn't be something you'd be interested in. You've never asked questions about it when any of us were talking about it at the pub or here at the compound."

The weights were getting heavier with each repetition, and Mike's muscles began to quiver, but he still had a few more in him. "Maybe it just took the right woman. Not that I'm . . . argghh . . . saying I'm definitely going to try this thing with her. But . . . arrrggghhhh . . . I have to admit, I'm attracted to her. I mean, she's hot as sin. I'd have to be on your end of the rainbow not to be fantasizing about her . . . arrrrrrrgggghhhhhhhh—enough!"

Jake quickly grasped the bar and helped set it into the cradle above the bench. Once it was safe to do so, Mike released it, shook out his exhausted arms, and stood, taking the towel Jake handed him to wipe the bench down. "I honestly don't know what I'm going to do, Jake. All I do know is I can't stop thinking about her . . . and her offer."

Spreading his legs shoulder-width apart and crossing his arms over his chest, in that manner all military men seem to do, Jake cocked his head to the side. "Look. I'm not trying to talk you into it or out of it—that's your decision—just remember that if you do decide to explore the lifestyle with her—or anyone else—there's going to be a contract in place—most likely one with an end date. That means, on that date, the fun and games may come to a grinding halt, and the two of you go back to being friends or acquaintances, or you sign another contract with another end date. This isn't the kind of dating you're used to, Mike—hell, Charlotte may not even call it dating. Just make sure you're going into this with your eyes wide open and no delusions that there's a wedding ring, house with a white picket fence, and two-point-four kids at the end of it if that's what you're looking for."

Mike nodded. "I get it—I do. Do I want those things somewhere down the line? Damn right, I do. Five years ago, I would have said no, but now that the big four-oh is approaching, what I want out of life has changed. Will I get that with Charlotte? Who knows? But I get the feeling, now that she's put the idea in my head, I'm not going to shake it until I see if what she's offering is for me."

"All right. As I said, the decision is yours. If you've got any questions, you can ask me or Nick. Otherwise, I promise I'll stay out of it."

"Thanks. And Jake?" He held out his hand. "Thanks for caring enough to risk pissing off a friend of yours because you're worried about me."

Taking Mike's hand, Jake pulled him into a bro-hug and slapped him on the back. "We've come a long way—just didn't want to lose what we've gained these past two years."

"Amen."

MIKE TOOK a deep breath and pushed "Send" on his cell phone. Putting it to his ear, he waited for the call to connect. He wasn't sure if he was happy or disappointed when it went to voicemail. At the sound of the beep, he cleared his throat and plunged ahead. "Hey . . . Hi . . . Charlotte, it's . . . uh . . . me . . . Mike . . . uh . . . Mike Donovan. I'm calling like you told me to, and . . . I . . . uh . . . was wondering if we could get together later and . . . talk, I guess. I'll be at the pub for a few hours tonight, so if you want, we can have dinner here and, I don't know . . . just talk. Give me a call and let me know." He rattled off his cell phone number just in case it didn't appear on her cell phone screen for some reason. "Uh . . . okay . . . bye."

Disconnecting the call, he mentally cursed himself for coming across as a blithering idiot. He couldn't remember the last time he'd sounded like a pre-pubescent boy calling a girl for the first time. Unfortunately, it was too late to take his message back.

"Excuse me, are you Mike Donovan?"

He glanced up to see a woman in her mid-thirties eyeing him. "Yes, can I help you?"

Her tentative expression morphed into a cheerful smile. She held out her hand. "Hi, I'm Daniella Mavis. I have an interview with you for the waitress position."

Mike had been so wrapped up in his thoughts about Charlotte that he hadn't realized a half hour had passed by so quickly. Shaking the woman's hand, he said, "It's nice to meet you. Why don't we sit in the party room in the back and talk? Can I get you something to drink?"

As she shook her head and answered, "No, thanks," Mike tried to force the thoughts of the hot Domme from his mind, which was hard to do—she was a helluva distraction. Play would come later, but for now, he had work to do.

Five

Standing, Charlotte circumvented her desk and walked out into the reception area, her gaze seeking out her next appointment among the dozen or so parolees and probationers waiting for their assigned officers. She spotted Jose Perez as he stood and strode toward her, a genuine smile on his face. Turning, Charlotte returned to her office with the young man on her heels.

Taking her seat again, she leaned back and stared at him. "I take it that smile means you got a job."

"Yes, ma'am. I did what you said and went to talk to that career counselor, and she found me a job in a restaurant, putting what I learned in prison to good use."

Charlotte couldn't help the grin that spread across her face. Despite turning to a life of crime to support his child and fiancée, he'd managed to hold on to the manners the grandmother who'd raised him had instilled in him. "That's great. Which restaurant?"

She grabbed his file and her pen to write down the information.

"It's a place called Donovan's Pub. The owner's really

cool. There's another guy who works in the kitchen who did time too."

Her hand froze with the pen's tip pressed against the page in his file as she tried to maintain the false smile that had replaced her real one. It took a moment for the shock to wear off at the mention of Mike Donovan's bar. Well, at least he'd hired a kid who really was trying to turn his life around. She hadn't known Mike had hired anyone from the ex-felon reintegration program sponsored by the state, but honestly, she wasn't too surprised after she thought about it. She could see him wanting to give a job to someone who was trying to straighten out their life. That was the type of guy he was.

On her desk, her cell phone vibrated with a new call, and she glanced at the screen. *Michael*. She let it go to voicemail, not wanting to take a personal call with a parolee in the room. She'd call him back in a few minutes. She fought the urge to grin as she wondered if he was sweating nervously, waiting for her to return his call.

Turning her attention back to the task at hand, she wrote "Donovan's Pub" down on the paper, then asked, "What hours are you working there?"

Jose rattled off his schedule, and Charlotte transcribed it. She'd have to do a drop-in at some point within the next two weeks to ensure all was well and that he, indeed, had the job. She could ask Mike, but doing things by the book was one of her fast rules. Besides, she didn't want to mix business and pleasure.

After Jose left, Charlotte saw two more appointments before shutting her office door and retrieving her voicemail. Excitement pooled low in her abdomen as she listened to Mike's hesitant message. His nervousness, combined with the sexy timber of his voice, was turning her on. While he hadn't said yes or no, she was almost positive he would accept her offer. It'd been several years since she'd played with a man new to the lifestyle, and she anticipated it more than she'd expected.

Saving the message, Charlotte hit the callback number and waited for him to pick up.

"Hello?"

"Hello, Michael. Dinner sounds wonderful. I'm looking forward to talking with you. What time is best for you? I don't want to interfere with your business . . . even if it is for pleasure," she added with a seductive purr.

There was a moment of silence, and she thought she heard him gulp before he finally answered her. "Um . . . is seven too late? It's after the dinner rush, so it's less likely we'll be interrupted."

"Seven is fine, Michael. I'll see you then. Goodbye."

"Goodbye, Charlotte."

Oh, yes. He's definitely going to accept my offer.

AT 7:00 p.m. on the nose, Mike almost swallowed his tongue as the front door to the pub swung open, and Charlotte sashayed in. Her skin-tight blue jeans, calf-high biker boots, and emerald green top caught the attention of every guy in the place—and a few women. Well, actually, it was probably the stunning woman who was in the clothes that had a bunch of them drooling—Charlotte Roth was mouthwatering. But she ignored everyone else for the most part, although she smiled and greeted a few people on her way down the bar to where Mike stood. She'd immediately sought him out and remained focused on his face as she approached.

Swallowing hard, Mike's gaze involuntarily dropped to the tips of her boots as they came closer and closer before stopping right in front of him.

"Good evening, Michael. How was your day?"

His eyes lifted again, and he found a sexy and slightly amused smile on her face. And just like that, his cock twitched—several times, in fact.

Come on, Donovan, get a grip.

"It was good. I hired a nice woman to take Jenn's position when she leaves. Can I get you something to drink?"

"A white-wine spritzer, please." As he went behind the bar to make her drink, she hopped up on one of the stools and hung her purse on one of the hooks he'd put under the lip of the bar for that purpose after a suggestion from Kristin Sawyer. As a guy, it never occurred to him that women were always trying to figure out the best place for their bags, where they were safe yet out of the way. "Shelby mentioned you're going to throw Jenn a going-away party."

Relieved they weren't just jumping into the heavy conversation that was coming, he grinned as he grabbed a bottle of white wine and a glass. "Word spreads fast. I only mentioned it to Shelby yesterday when she and Parker brought the boys in for lunch. It won't be a fancy thing, but a lot of her regulars will be stopping in, and friends and family are invited, of course, including you. Kristen and Angie offered to notify everyone this week. We'll just set up a buffet and have an open bar for a while. She deserves a party—everyone loves her here."

"She's a sweet girl. She'll do well in social work."

Setting Charlotte's drink in front of her, he snatched another glass and poured himself a club soda. "Yeah, she really likes it." He shot a glance at her. "So, how was your day?"

"Long, as usual. But a certain voicemail I received made it much more enjoyable."

A blush stole across Mike's cheeks. *Damn, how does she do that to me? I never blush!*

"I'm looking forward to our discussion about your decision, but first, there's something else I need to tell you. Can we go into the party room where we won't be overheard?"

Mike's stomach quivered, and he tried to remind himself nothing would happen between them here. The doors to the party room were open, and anyone could look in and see them. "Ah, sure." He grabbed a menu and a list of specials. "Why don't you let me know what you want to eat first, and I'll put in the order. Someone will bring it into us."

"Are you joining me? I hate to eat alone when I'm with someone."

Trying to ignore how jealous it made him feel thinking about this gorgeous woman having dinner with another guy, Mike took a sip of his drink before answering her. "I haven't had dinner yet, so yes, I'll join you."

"Good." She quickly perused the specials. "The salmon looks delicious, but instead of rice, I'll take a double helping of the vegetables, if you don't mind."

"Not at all. Soup or salad with it?"

"No, thank you."

Taking the menus back, he jotted down her order on a pad and added his before handing it to one of the waitresses. Since Mike wouldn't charge Charlotte for the dinner, it would only screw up the night's receipts if he entered it into the computer. Picking up his and Charlotte's drinks, he canted his head toward the unoccupied room. "Shall we?"

She gave him a broad smile that caused butterflies to take flight in his stomach and his cock to twitch again. Retrieving her purse, she stood and led the way with Mike's gaze glued to her shapely ass. He wasn't surprised when she sat at a table toward the back of the room facing the door to the bar. The only other door in the room was an emergency exit that had no handle on the outside. With her career as a state parole officer, Charlotte clearly had the same instincts that Mike had observed in Jake and his coworkers. None of them liked to sit with their backs to a room or door.

Setting the drinks on the table, Mike sat across from Charlotte. Now that they were alone, he had no idea what to say. Thankfully, she didn't have the same problem. "I usually don't mix business with pleasure, but I can't avoid it this time. I understand you recently hired an ex-felon, Jose Perez, to work in your kitchen."

Mike's eyes narrowed in alarm. "I did. Is he trouble?"

"No, not at all. I actually don't think he'll be a repeat offender. I just want you to know I'm his parole officer, and I'll be doing an occasional drop-in to see how he's doing. Most of my visits are to the parolees' homes, but I will do one or two at their job sites. I wasn't sure if you knew that and thought you should know before I do my first one. I haven't told Jose you and I are acquainted, but he'll inevitably see me here, off duty, at some point."

His shoulders relaxed again. "Thanks for the warning, but Jose isn't the first guy I've hired from the career program. There were two others—one worked out, the other didn't. For what it's worth, he's been doing great this past week. He learned a lot in the prison kitchen and is picking up the routine here quickly. He hasn't given me or the staff any problems. In fact, my evening chef, Tommy, said Jose is ten times better than the last guy. In this business, it's wise to keep your chef happy."

"I'm sure." She leaned back in her chair and rested her hands on her lap. "Now that business is out of the way, let's focus on pleasure. Have you decided about exploring the lifestyle with me, Michael?"

Her confident expression told Mike she already knew what his answer would be, but it didn't make it any easier to say it. He shifted on the chair, more from her scrutiny than the seat itself being uncomfortable. "I . . . uh . . . yes . . . I did. But I have a bunch of questions first."

"Okay. Shoot."

"Um . . . all right. The first question is about a contract. Jake said we'd have a contract between us with . . . um . . . an end date."

She raised an eyebrow in curiosity, not annoyance like he'd expected. "You and Jake talked about you and me?"

"Yeah. He told me he went to see you and stuck his nose where it didn't belong. But he didn't try to talk me out of it if that's what you're asking. He just wanted to make sure I knew what I was getting into, then promised to stay out of it."

"What you're getting into . . . so, that means your answer is yes?"

It took him a moment to realize he hadn't actually said yes to her yet, and that she needed to hear it. "Uh . . . yes, I'll admit, I'm curious and interested, but like I said, I have questions."

"I'd worry if you didn't. So, the answer to question number one is yes, we'll have a contract. It will spell out exactly what I expect from you, what you can expect from me, what our hard limits are, and yes, there will be an end date, one month from the day we sign the contract. On the end date, *if*, by mutual agreement, we want to renew the contract, with or without any amendments, we will."

"Okay, I can deal with that." After talking to Jake and Nick and researching more, that was the answer he'd expected to hear from her, which is why he'd started with that question. Now for the harder ones. "Um . . . I guess the next question is . . . um . . . are you going to want to degrade and humiliate me? I read some Dominants get off on that . . . the subs too. I'm not too keen on that."

"Which is why we'll negotiate your hard and soft limits."

Reaching into her purse, she pulled out several folded pages and opened them. "This is a limit list, and most items on it are negotiable with me, Michael. You'll know full well which ones aren't before we both sign the bottom of the contract. If public humiliation is not your thing, then I'm willing to abide by that—it's not one of my favorite parts of the lifestyle anyway, but some subs crave it. However, that being said, there are some acts you might think are humiliating, while I believe they're a sign of your respect and submission."

He leaned on his forearms crossed atop the table. "Such as?"

"Such as, I would expect you to kneel in a presenting position when instructed. That would be with your knees shoulder-width apart, head bowed, and hands clasped around your forearms behind your lower back. Mind you, it wouldn't be all the time—only during play—and it's something Nick does with Jake, in case you're wondering. In other words, it's not unusual in the lifestyle." She paused. "Do you have a problem with that?"

He took a moment to consider it and think of it from her point of view. "No, I don't think it'll be a problem—as long as it's done in private."

The corners of Charlotte's mouth ticked upward. "I would expect it more than just in private, Michael. It would also be in public at the club."

His eyebrows shot up. "Th-the club? We'd be going to The Covenant?"

"Not at first, but yes, at some point, I'll want to take you to the club."

Okay, he hadn't expected she'd want him to go to the BDSM club with her. In fact, he'd never been inside it, even though he'd been to the Trident Security compound many times.

"And I promise," she continued, "that you and Nick will

not be the only two alpha-submissive males there. There are quite a few."

"Alpha-submissive? What's that?"

Charlotte's smile widened as her gaze roamed his arms, shoulders, and chest appreciatively. "Men . . . or women, who have alpha personalities everywhere other than the bedroom. It's more common than people suspect, and there's absolutely nothing wrong with it."

Suddenly a flash of jealousy coursed through him, and he wondered how many of those alpha-submissive men Charlotte had been with. Thankfully, she didn't seem to pick up on his thoughts.

"I'll give you plenty of notice before we go, and we won't be able to play there until your application is completed and a health exam is done. In fact, that's another thing we have to talk about. I'll require you to wear a condom whenever we play and for you to schedule a complete physical with your doctor within the next week. I have a copy of my own recent physical for you as well."

Charlotte paused, and Mike was about to ask another question but slammed his mouth shut when he realized one of the waitresses had entered the room, carrying their dinners. He sat back from the table so she could set the plates down. "Thanks, Claire."

"No problem. Do you need anything else?"

Mike didn't, and he eyed Charlotte, who shook her head and responded, "No, thank you. This looks and smells wonderful."

"Enjoy."

As Claire left them alone, Charlotte picked up her fork and took a bite of her salmon. Her perfect, red lips opened and then closed around the morsel. Her eyelids fluttered shut, and she let out a small, satisfied moan. "Mmm. Delicious."

This time his cock did more than just twitch inside his jeans. It swelled. Never in his life had Mike thought of watching a woman eat as foreplay, but damn, Charlotte was turning him on. If he didn't get control of himself, he'd be on his knees before she was halfway through her meal, begging her to do whatever she wanted to him.

Six

They ate in comfortable silence for a few minutes before Mike wiped his mouth with his napkin. "Is it okay if I ask you some more questions?"

Charlotte fought the urge to grin. His submissiveness shone through, loud and clear, though she doubted he was aware of it. "Of course, Michael. What else would you like to know?"

"Well, this is sort of a big one." He took a deep breath and let it out in a rush. "It's about the whip. Is that something you'll want to do with me? Because, honestly, just the thought of it freaks me out."

She let the question hang in the air momentarily as she speared a honey-glazed carrot and ate it. With most of her dinner gone and her stomach full, she set the fork down, picked up her wine spritzer, and leaned back in her chair, crossing her legs.

Charlotte decided to give Mike some of her background before answering him. "During my junior year of college, I was dating a guy for a few weeks when he finally confessed he was submissive and drawn to my dominant nature. Until then, I didn't know I *had* a dominant nature. As you just said, it freaked me out when he told me he was into pain for pleasure and wanted me to use a crop on him. But after my initial shock, I decided to keep an open mind and let him take me to a munch, so I could talk to others in the lifestyle and see if it was for me.

"While, eventually, he and I went our separate ways, I'd found a home in the community. Things I didn't know were deep inside me came to the surface, but once they did, I couldn't figure out how I'd done without them until then. So, I began to research everything I could find. I asked several Dominants to mentor me—first as a submissive and then as a Mistress.

"To put it in a way for you to really understand, it's like starting to learn a business from the ground up. I remember you saying here one night that when you started working for your father, your first job was as a dishwasher. Then when you mastered that, you moved on to busboy, then waiter, then the chef's assistant, and bartender. He made sure you knew every job necessary to make this a successful business."

Mike grimaced. "Yeah, he might have been a bastard when it came to being a father, but he knew how to run a restaurant and trained me well. One of the few good things he did for me."

Charlotte's heart skipped a beat, and she fought the urge to comfort him—he wasn't ready for that and might mistake it for pity. Instead, she complimented him. "And you've done a wonderful job with the place. You took what he taught you and then added to it, making it even better than it was."

She knew it was because of Mike that the place now had computerized ordering, new menus and dinner choices, a softball team with the pub's name on their uniforms, and Monday and Tuesday night dart teams. Sean Donovan had apparently hated change and had turned down every suggestion his eldest son had made to upgrade the place.

Charlotte hadn't known the older man and had never been in the pub until after he'd died and Mike had taken over, but from what she'd heard from longtime customers, the changes had been welcome improvements.

"Thanks."

Damn, she loved that sweet blush on his cheeks. It was clear he wasn't used to taking compliments—when they started to play, she planned to rectify that. Part of being a Domme was ensuring the sub knew their worth, and never in a negative sense. Charlotte had a feeling it would take much subtle and direct coaxing on her part for him to realize he was a very fine man in every way.

"You're welcome." She took a sip of her drink. "Now, back to what I was talking about. Training to be a submissive before becoming a Dominant goes beyond knowing the 'jobs' of a sub. It helps a Dom learn what a sub will be thinking and feeling during play, and that will help build a crucial connection between the two.

"The lifestyle isn't just about mastering the physical aspects between a Dom and sub, but also the emotional ones that only a few can hope to achieve. If anyone tells you they're in the lifestyle because of their physical needs only, then they're in it for the wrong reasons. Mental and emotional satisfaction should always come before physical satisfaction. That's what many people don't understand."

She paused a moment to study his non-verbal response to the information. It appeared he was still following her and not confused, so she continued. "Now, despite what many submissives at the club think, what I want them to think, I'm not as much of a sadist as I portray. Yes, I know how to dole out pain for pleasure, but I mainly learned so I could give my submissives what they needed. Not everyone is wired that way, Michael. I need to give my sub what *he* needs, and if that involves pain, then that's what I'll give him.

"As for punishments, that's something different altogether. I've learned to get creative. There are plenty of alternatives for discipline that I've come up with that don't involve pain. In fact, I'm quite sure once you've experienced some of them, you'll be looking for ways to earn more punishments." She smiled and winked at him. Curiosity and lust flared in his eyes, fueling her own desire. "I see you're eager to learn what those are, but I'll keep them to myself for now."

She loved the mind games involved in BDSM—they heightened the attraction between her and the submissive, and the anticipation of what was to come was one of the biggest aphrodisiacs she'd ever known.

Picking up the papers she'd taken from her purse, she handed them to him. "Before we start to play, I want you to fill out the limit list. Green is for activities you're willing to participate in without any hesitation. Yellow is for ones you've never tried or have had limited experience with that you're willing to explore. Red is for hard limits—those you have no desire to engage in. Don't overthink this, Michael. There are things on this list that don't appeal to me either. We'll go over my list after you've completed yours. I don't want my soft and hard limits to influence you while you go through these. Be honest with yourself—and with me. If there are any items on the list you're not sure about and want to discuss before assigning a color, then leave them blank for now. Understood?"

His gaze skimmed the top page before he nodded. "Understood." He hesitated a moment before adding, "So . . . what happens now?"

Damn, he's so cute. His uncertainty had her wanting to take him into his office and blow his mind, among other things. But that would have to wait.

Standing, she hooked her purse onto her arm and moved beside him. She knew the moment he realized she was leaving, and before he could get to his feet, she grabbed a handful of his hair and yanked his head back. Excitement coursed through her when she saw shock and pain morph into lust and need in his eyes.

Bending down, she gently brushed her lips against his, her hold on his head preventing him from closing the distance between them. She was in control, and it would take time for him to immediately surrender to her whenever she demanded it. As his education continued, he'd learn the benefits and rewards of prompt submission.

"Tomorrow night, you'll come to my house at 7:00 p.m. sharp—not a minute later—and we'll go over your limit list, which I want you to complete tonight before you go to bed. During the day tomorrow, I want you to do some homework." His eyes narrowed slightly. "Yes, my dear, homework. I want you to research what happens when a male orgasms. When you report to me tomorrow night, you'll need to be able to explain exactly what happens in the male body—physically, emotionally, and mentally—before, during, and after his sexual release. Understood?"

When he tried to nod, her grip prevented it. "No, Michael. I insist on a verbal answer whenever I ask you a question, followed by my title—Ma'am or Mistress if we're alone or in the club. In public, where we won't be advertising the dynamics of our relationship, you may call me Charlotte. While you're my submissive, you will also not refer to me as Mistress China—that title is for those I'm not in a contracted relationship with. Now, let's try this again. Do you understand what your homework assignment is and what I expect you to explain to me tomorrow night?"

He swallowed hard before answering, his voice rasping across every nerve of her skin, causing them to tingle. "Yes, I understand, Mistress."

She skimmed her lips against his again. They were soft and supple, and it took all her strength to pull away and not ravage him. "Very good, Michael. I'll see you tomorrow then. Have a good night, and remember, that hard-on you're currently sporting is mine. You're not to touch it unless I allow it. I'll know if you do, and you won't like the punishment."

Letting go of his hair, she turned on her heel and walked out the door, smiling to herself.

Seven

Glancing around the bar, Mike made sure there was nothing else that needed his attention before heading home to shower and change. The last thing he wanted to do was to show up at Charlotte's late. She'd sent him a text earlier with her home address. He'd actually been surprised since Nick had said that, as far as he knew, Mistress China rarely played outside of the club. But Mike had been relieved she wasn't throwing him to the wolves, so to speak, by taking him directly to The Covenant. He had no idea how that would go over with the men he knew that belonged to the club. With Nick as a sub there, he doubted they'd say anything to embarrass Mike, but that didn't mean he still wouldn't feel it.

The new waitress, Daniella, walked up to the bar. "Hey, Mike, can I get a chardonnay and a Coke, please?"

Since the bartender, Missy, was busy at the other end, Mike grabbed two glasses to fill the order. "Sure. How's everything going? You're picking things up quickly."

Indeed, she was. He'd been a little surprised . . . okay, a lot surprised, when she'd handed him her resume. During the past few years, she'd been a homemaker, before that, she'd worked for some of the most prestigious restaurants on the gulf coast of Florida. And not as a waitress, but she had, literally, run the dining rooms—everything from handling the staff, hosting parties and wine pairing events and making sure the atmosphere was just right. In other words, she was completely overqualified for the job.

Her response to his incredulity was that she was going through a divorce, and since she hadn't worked in years, her connections had dried up, and there weren't many places that could hire someone with her experience. The ones that could weren't in the market for a dining room manager, so she was taking what she could get. Jenn had been training her, but aside from pointing out where things were and how to work the new ordering computer, there wasn't much she needed to learn. Daniella had even won over Harvey, the daytime chef, in no time, which was almost unheard of.

"It's going well. You've got a great setup here, and Jenn is a sweetheart. I can tell she's really going to miss working here."

"She is great but was never going to be a lifer. She's really looking forward to a career in social work—it fits her personality, too. And since her uncles are in here all the time, I'm sure she'll be stopping by so much we won't have a chance to miss her."

When he handed over her drinks, Daniella thanked him and then brought them to her customers. The front door opened, and two of his evening staff members walked in, causing Mike to check the clock. He had two hours before he had to be at Charlotte's, but he wanted to stop by his mother's house first. He and Jake would sit down and talk with her tomorrow about the assisted living facility. Mike was hoping she'd at least agree to look at the place. If her memory worsened, they'd rather she already be there. It would probably be less stressful for all of them.

Saying goodbye to his employees and telling them to call if he was needed, he grabbed the takeout container Jenn had prepared for him and shook hands with a few regulars on his way to the door. Less than ten minutes later, he pulled into the driveway of the house he'd grown up in. He had a love/hate relationship with the place. His childhood had been good, if uneventful, until Mike's early teen years when Sean Donovan became more interested in Jake becoming a professional football player than anything else. From the time one of the Pop Warner coaches had told Sean that, with the proper guidance, his youngest son had the potential to go all the way to the pros one day, everything the family had done revolved around Jake's training and games.

While he loved his brother, Mike couldn't help but know he was second best in his father's eyes, and the boy he'd been had resented it. But he'd grown up so much since then. Not only physically but emotionally. He was just grateful he'd been able to mend his torn relationship with his brother recently. It hadn't been Jake's fault their father had been an arrogant, selfish bigot. In fact, in the end, Jake had become persona non-grata in Sean's eyes because of his homosexuality, which, itself, had never bothered Mike. He'd always regret telling their father in a moment of jealous weakness, but as Jake had said to him, the past is in the past. He needed to put that all behind him and enjoy the future.

Using his own key to let himself into the house, he wasn't too surprised to see his mother's neighbor there. A little younger than Emma Donovan, Linda Baker had befriended her when she'd moved in next door about three years ago. She knew what it was like to be a widow, and the two women had been able to commiserate with each other. It gave Mike and Jake an extra set of eyes on their mother and a backup in case neither of them was available in an emergency—which was rare but possible.

The two women looked up from their perches on the couch where they were having some tea. Linda was the first to greet him. "Hi, Mike."

"Hi, Linda. Hi, Mom."

"Oh, hi, Michael, I didn't expect you home from school this early. Was your class canceled?"

Oh boy. It's one of those days.

His gaze flitted to Linda's sympathetic one before returning to his mother's worn face. When had it gotten so wrinkled? "Mom, I've been out of school a long time, remember?"

She shook her head and waved a hand in the air as her memory cleared. "Oh, I'm sorry. I forgot. Linda and I were just talking about when our children were young, and I got caught up in the moment. How was work, dear?"

"Good." He raised his hand, letting her see the takeout container. "Harvey made you some chicken piccata for dinner. There's plenty, Linda, if you'd like to have some too."

The woman stood and took it from him. "Sounds wonderful. I'll put it in the kitchen, and we'll reheat it in a little while. Sit with your mom for a minute while I make us another cup of tea. Would you like one?"

She knew the answer to that, but it was nice that she always asked. "No, thanks."

When she left the room, Mike took her place on the couch beside his mother. "How was your day?"

"It was okay. I was feeling a little lonely before Linda came over. There's no one else around anymore."

That was one of the things she complained about often, but when either Jake or Mike brought up the topic of an assisted living facility, she usually balked. Biting his tongue,

Mike didn't get into that discussion with her again. It could wait until tomorrow when he had reinforcements. "Well, why don't I come get you for lunch tomorrow? Jake and Nick are coming by the restaurant to talk about Jenn's farewell party."

"Jenn's leaving? I didn't know she was moving."

"She's not, Mom. She's got an internship for college, and then she'll be looking for a job in social work." That was the fifth or sixth time in the past week he'd told her that.

"Oh, good. She's such a nice girl. You should ask her out now that she won't be working for you."

Looks like she forgot the huge age difference between Jenn and me and that Jake's a surrogate uncle to her. "She's dating someone, Mom."

He didn't know if that was true, but it got his mother off the matchmaking topic. "That's too bad. But lunch sounds wonderful. Will Jake and Nick be there?"

Yup, and I just said that less than a minute ago.

"They'll be there." As Linda returned to the room, Mike stood and then gave his mother a peck on the cheek. "I'll pick you up at noon tomorrow."

"Oh, you don't have to—I can drive myself."

His eyes flashed to Linda, who subtly canted her head toward the kitchen. It was clear that Emma was worse today than usual, and the other woman needed to tell him something. Leaving his mother on the couch, he followed Linda into the other room.

When they were out of earshot, she pulled two sets of keys from her pocket. "I'm worried about her. She tried to back the car out of the driveway earlier and couldn't do it. She ran over the garbage cans and then ended up hopping the curb across the street and driving up onto the Hodges' lawn. I convinced her to let me park the car back in the driveway, then took her to the store in my car. I swiped her car keys. The second set I took from the table in the foyer. I didn't know what else to do."

Mike grimaced. "Damn. Thanks for taking care of her." He pocketed the keys. "Hopefully, she'll think she misplaced them for now. Jake and I will talk to her about the assisted living facility tomorrow and take her over to see the place."

Patting his arm, Linda gave him a sympathetic smile. "I know it's hard, and I'll miss having her as a neighbor, but it's for the best. I'll be more than happy to visit her there, though. If you need help with anything, you let me know."

"Thanks, Linda. Jake and I really appreciate all you've done for Mom."

"She's a wonderful woman. I love spending time with her."

Returning to the living room, Mike gave his mother another kiss on the cheek and said goodbye to both women. Ten minutes later, he pulled into his condo complex. During the drive over, he'd called Jake and filled him in on what Linda had told him. Once that was done, he was able to put his mother out of his mind for a bit and think about Charlotte and their . . . date? Mike wasn't sure if that was the word for it. It wasn't exactly a date, and a meeting sounded too professional. Rendezvous? Tryst? Whatever it was, he was certainly looking forward to it.

After showering, he dressed in a gray polo shirt and a new pair of jeans. Sitting in the recliner in front of his widescreen TV, he reread the research he'd done for the "homework" Charlotte had given him. When his mother had asked about school earlier, the sexy Domme had flashed in his mind. She'd been wearing all black—a leather skirt, lacy bra, and thigh-high boots while cracking a whip. Not an image he wanted to be salivating over while standing in front of the woman who'd given birth to him.

Once he was pretty sure he remembered everything, he

folded the piece of paper with his notes on it and stuffed it into his back pocket—just in case he forgot something. Grabbing his keys, wallet, phone, and almost completed limit list, he headed out the door. Using the GPS in his truck's dash, it didn't take him long to reach Charlotte's house.

At the back of a quiet cul-de-sac, her small, one-floor ranch sat on a lot that was about three-quarters of an acre. A fence enclosed the backyard, and two lines of trees created a barrier between her property and the neighbors on either side. There were no vehicles in the driveway or the street directly in front of the house, and he assumed she parked the SUV he knew she drove in the garage.

Glancing at his truck's radio, he noted the time. He was six minutes early. Parking in the street, he turned off the ignition and took a deep breath. He couldn't remember the last time he'd been nervous about being with a woman—not since he'd been a teenager, a very long time ago. But that nervousness wasn't a bad thing. In fact, he was semi-hard just thinking about seeing her again, not to mention finding out what she had planned for him tonight.

Climbing out of the car, he strode up the driveway. The sky to the west behind the house was filled with slashes of reds, oranges, and yellows as the sun prepared to set. It looked like a painter had used the horizon as his latest canvas.

Mike's heart pounded in his chest as he raised his hand and rang the doorbell. In the silence around him, he heard the clicking of heels on tiles on the other side of the door—they were slow and methodical, and he imagined Charlotte sashaying seductively down a hallway. The door was unlocked and then opened. As he seemed to be prone to doing whenever he was near this woman as of late, Mike almost choked on his tongue.

Charlotte was dressed in a black, skin-tight catsuit that

hugged every curve of her delectable body. A zipper on her chest was lowered to give him an enticing view of her cleavage. The black, thigh-high boots he'd imagined earlier covered her legs. Her shiny black hair hung straight down below her shoulders, and subtle makeup enhanced her facial features.

She really was a stunning woman, and for the first time since all this started, Mike wondered what the hell she saw in him. He wasn't anything special to look at—not that he was ugly. He'd had his fair share of women flirt with him, but with Charlotte, he couldn't help but feel she was way out of his league.

"Hello, Michael," she purred. "Welcome to my home. Please, come in."

Swallowing hard, he stepped inside before she closed the door behind him. His gaze darted around the place Charlotte owned and lived in. He wasn't sure what he'd expected, but the comfortable, earth-toned decor hadn't been it.

When she passed by him and walked down the hall toward the kitchen, the sway of her hips demanded all his attention as he followed. While he was still on edge, his lust for this woman was quickly taking over his body. Never in his adult life had he wanted to beg a woman for anything, but with Charlotte, begging was something he was now looking forward to.

Eight

Charlotte led her new sub into the kitchen, then turned on her heel to face him.

Damn, he looks delicious.

"Can I get you something to drink? Water? Soda? I won't offer you anything stronger since we'll be playing at some point this evening."

"Um . . . water . . . water will be fine. Thank you."

Taking two glasses from a cabinet, she filled them from the tap in her refrigerator. "Take deep breaths, Michael. I'm not going to pounce on you. We're going to sit and talk for a little while."

She handed him one of the glasses, then gestured to the home's family room. "Please, take a seat on the couch." She'd specifically indicated where she wanted him to sit. If she'd given him a choice, she was sure he'd try to put some distance between them and sit in one of the two recliners.

As the soft jazz music she had on filtered through the air, her pure black cat decided to grace the newcomer with his presence and emerged from wherever he'd been hiding after the doorbell had rung. Confucius jumped onto the ottoman in front of where Mike had taken a seat and meowed loudly at him. Mike chuckled, and some of the tension in his shoulders eased a little as he reached out and scratched the feline's ears. "A black cat, huh? Is there a bit of witch mixed in with your sadistic Domme persona?"

Smiling, Charlotte sat beside him and curled her legs under her as she faced him. "Maybe. But I didn't plan on ever having a cat. My family always had dogs while I was growing up. I found Confucius by accident. When he was a kitten, some heartless ass had left him in a box next to the shopping carts at the grocery store I use. I took one look at those amber-colored eyes and fell in love. I've been his mistress ever since. He's the only one I'll ever submit to, and he knows it, the little brat."

The cat meowed and then purred loudly in response.

"Confucius? Interesting name," Mike said, relaxing back on the couch, his gaze turning to hers.

"Mm-hmm. He taught the virtues of order, structure, and correct behavior—things I like to have in my life." Resting her elbow on the back of the couch, she lightly caressed his shoulder. "Things I *need* in my life. I've noticed that about you too. When you're working, you do certain things the same way every time, as if you'll miss something if you do it otherwise."

"Really? I've never noticed."

"I notice a lot of things about you, Michael. It makes me wonder why I never noticed your submissiveness before now."

He sipped his water before placing it on a coaster on the side table next to him. "Maybe because I had no clue I had it in me."

"Perhaps. But whatever the reason, I'm glad it finally came to my attention." She handed him her glass. "Please put that next to yours." She didn't ask him if he wouldn't mind doing the small task, wanting him to get used to following her commands for simple things. It would help when she upped the ante.

Dropping the hand that had been holding the glass to his knee, Charlotte made lazy circles with her fingers. His leg muscles tightened, and she could tell he was trying to hold onto the control she wanted him to give over to her. In time, it would become second nature to him, but for now, it was the beginning of his training. "So, tell me, Michael, what did you learn about the male orgasm?"

"Um, what do you want to know?"

"My directive to you was to research everything that happens to a man before, during, and after an orgasm, so that's exactly what I want to know. And since you're new to this, and I wasn't entirely clear, we've moved into D/s mode, which means you will address me by my title as I've already instructed." Her fingers at his shoulder trailed to the skin of his nape that was exposed above his shirt. She was thrilled when a shiver coursed through him.

"Right, um . . . I mean, yes, Ma'am." He took a shuddering breath. "Right, the male orgasm." When he said that last word, the hand on his knee moved an inch or so up his leg, and he gulped before letting out a nervous laugh. "I feel like I'm back in my high school health class. Okay . . . um, when something or someone prompts a sexual interest in a man, the brain sends out a signal down the spine to the . . . sexual organs."

"Michael," Charlotte interrupted, her hand moving further toward the growing bulge in his groin in a sensual seduction, "my fingers aren't very far away from those sexual organs of yours, so you may use the words cock and balls or any others you want. You don't need to sound like a textbook. In fact, I prefer you don't. Dirty talk while playing isn't considered crass in my book."

"Um . . . right . . . um . . . yes, Ma'am." His gaze dropped to her hand on his leg. Taking a deep breath, he then let it out and forged ahead. "Where was I? Um, the brain sends a signal to . . . the cock, which then gets hard with five times the normal amount of blood rushing . . ." He inhaled sharply as her fingers moved higher, about an inch from his erection. "Uh . . . blood rushing to it. Jesus, Charlotte—"

"Tsk, tsk." She brought her hand back to his knee. "Forgetting to use my title will delay any relief you're hoping for."

"Shit . . . um. Sorry, Ma'am."

Charlotte smirked. "Very good, Michael. Continue."

As her fingers started moving in small circles again, his chin lifted until his head hit the back of the couch. "Cha—I mean, Ma'am. May I adjust myself first? Things are getting very uncomfortable."

She hadn't expected him to ask permission so soon in their play—most subs forgot until they were reminded several times, which usually involved a punishment. "You obviously did a lot of research. That pleases me, and since you asked so nicely, yes, you may adjust yourself. But without using your hands. That hard-on is mine tonight."

Groaning, he shifted his hips, moving his ass closer to the edge of the couch, and reclined into a more comfortable position.

"Comfy?" When he nodded, Charlotte prompted, "Verbal responses, Michael."

His gaze met hers, and she saw heated lust in his eyes. The pulse in his neck was pounding as he licked his lips. "Yes, Ma'am."

"Good. Take a drink of your water if you need it, then continue."

Lifting her glass, he glanced at her. Pride swelled within her. "No, thank you, Michael. I'm good for the moment."

Taking his glass, he gulped half of it before putting it back down. He seemed to draw on some inner strength before speaking again. "Okay. Erection. Blood. Veins at the base of the cock squeeze shut, keeping the blood in so it stays hard. The balls get drawn up as the body's muscles tense. It takes the body between thirty seconds and two minutes to prepare for the orgasm. During that time, the pelvis begins to thrust involuntarily. The guy's breathing and heart rate increase. He feels like he's going to explode. When he reaches the point of no return, he'll come whether he wants to or not. Cum shoots out in a series of fast contractions of the muscles in the cock and ass. The nerves causing the muscles to contract send messages of pleasure to the brain, which by now is just a pile of mush. After he shoots his load, the erection fades. The muscles in the body relax, and he'll feel drowsy afterward."

During the rest of his explanation, Charlotte's hand got closer and closer to his bulging cock, which twitched in response to her ministrations. She was certain it wouldn't take much to send him over the edge into oblivion.

"That was very good, Michael. Thank you." She really couldn't care less about the hows and whys of the male orgasm at this moment, but it had been an exercise to see how much he was willing to invest in their relationship. She also wanted him to be comfortable in his own skin. And now that he'd pleased her, it was time to reward him. "Now, stand and strip completely."

His hazel gaze shot to hers as if he were shocked by her order before he stood and did as instructed. He'd probably been on the verge of begging for relief and was now silently hoping it was within reach. Turning, Charlotte grabbed a large throw pillow from the end of the couch and tossed it on the floor in front of her. Confucius stretched on the ottoman and then hopped down. Showing his furry ass, he strolled out of the room, appearing too dignified to watch his mistress play with her sub.

As Mike quickly shed his clothes and draped them over the arm of her recliner, Charlotte's gaze roamed his body, and her mouth watered. He had a typical Floridian man's tan on his upper torso, while his hips and legs were paler. She knew he mowed the lawn at his mother's house on a regular basis, and probably did it shirtless.

A swath of fine hair covered his chest and narrowed as it went lower to his groin, where a very impressive cock extended upward. On the tip was a bead of pre-cum that Charlotte intended to claim as hers. But it would have to wait for the moment.

She turned her attention to his next task. "Hand me your limit list, please."

After he pulled the folded paper from his pants pocket and gave it to her, she added, "Now, fold your clothes neatly and set them on the seat of the recliner."

His brow climbed a bit, but he silently obeyed the order. Charlotte wondered if Nick had drilled into his future brother-in-law the benefits of following a Dominant's commands without hesitation. As soon as he was done with his clothing, she pointed to the spot on the other side of the pillow on the floor. "Stand in front of me and present yourself—spread your feet shoulder-width apart, bow your head, and clasp your arms with your hands behind your lower back."

Once he was in the proper position, Charlotte set his limit list to the side and stood. Circling him, she ran her hands up his arms, across his back and chest, then lower to his ass and hips, avoiding his family jewels. She loved the mind games, which built up the anticipation for a sub. It made the results of a scene that much more enjoyable. Under his soft skin, his hard muscles quivered under her palms, and his breathing increased.

When he leaned into her touch, she removed her hands. "While we're in D/s mode, Michael, you must ask permission to speak or move. However, if something feels wrong, tell me immediately. Understood?"

"Yeah. I mean, yes, Ma'am."

"Your safeword is 'red.' If you're uncomfortable with a command or scene, say 'red,' and we'll stop and discuss what's wrong. Understood?"

There was only a moment's hesitation before he answered her. "Yes, Ma'am."

"Good. Kneel and present on the pillow, please. Rest back on your heels for comfort."

Somewhat ungracefully, Mike lowered himself onto his knees. When she was pleased with his posture, Charlotte sat down on the couch in front of him, then picked up and unfolded the papers he'd given her. Scanning the list, she was pleased to see most of their hard limits were similar, and there were quite a few things under the yellow column, meaning he hadn't tried them yet but was willing to. She smiled when she reached the second page and saw a ménage with two women in that column—typical male. Charlotte had no problem letting a female sub join them occasionally, but it would only be for Michael—she wasn't into women, although she had scened with many without sex involved. "The activities you didn't assign a color to we'll discuss during a visit to the club. I'll let you observe those scenes, and then you can decide if you're willing to try them or not."

"Thank you, Ma'am."

Charlotte put the list aside and stood again. Setting her hand on his upper arm, she trailed her fingers up to his shoulder, across his back, and down the other side. "You're a very fine male specimen, Michael."

A soft snort escaped him. "My brother got the looks in the family."

Grabbing his hair, Charlotte yanked his head back and glared at him, letting him see her annoyance about his words. "You will never, ever put yourself down or negatively compare yourself to anyone again, Michael. I won't stand for it. I wasn't only referring to you physically but also mentally and emotionally. You're strong, smart, sensitive, caring, and so much more. And, yes, you're physically attractive. All that combined makes for a very enticing package."

A package she couldn't wait any longer to experience. Bending, Charlotte slammed their mouths together. After a split second of surprise, Mike recovered and returned the kiss. His lips parted for her tongue, allowing her entry. Charlotte reveled in the taste of him—minty and spicy and all male. Her fingers in his hair held his head where she wanted it while her other hand explored his bare chest. She tweaked his nipples before scratching her way down his abdomen. Mike swayed, and his arm shot out and grabbed her around her hips to regain his balance.

Lifting her head enough to speak, Charlotte said, "You may hold onto me, but do nothing more than that. Tonight is about me showing you how much you've pleased me. You're going to come for me. I'll take my pleasure from seeing you lose control."

His eyes narrowed. "You don't want—"

"No." Reaching down, she wrapped her hand around his cock, causing him to hiss and moan in response. "This is what I want, Michael." Tightening her hold on the hard flesh, she explored the length. His hips bucked forward. "Uh-uh. Control the urge to do that. I'll let you know when you're allowed to."

Charlotte sat on the couch again, stretching her legs out on either side of her sub, never once releasing his cock. She swirled her hand around the thick stalk from its root to tip. Up, over, down, and back again. His every moan was hers. Every expression of ecstasy, every gasp, every response belonged to her. Using a finger from her other hand, she swiped it over his slit, taking some of the pre-cum, as she continued his sweet torture. "Eyes on me, Michael."

His eyelids were heavy as his gaze met hers. Opening her mouth, she brought her finger to her lips and licked it. "Mmm. Very nice."

Her hand dropped again, and she cupped his balls, gently rolling them in her hand. His legs began to quake, and she knew he was getting close. "Fuck my hand, subbie. Get ready to come for me—your orgasm is mine."

In time with her hand, Mike thrust his hips forward and back. "Jesus, that feels amazing. Oh, fuck! Char—Ma'am. Please!"

"It feels amazing to me too." She studied his face and body language. His moaning vibrated through the air, and she felt it in her core. "Do you want to come, Michael?"

"Oh, God, yes!"

Charlotte's hands froze. "What did you say?"

His eyes went wide as his hips stilled. She could see frustration and agitation surging through them. The muscles in his jaw, arms, abs, and thighs tightened as his mind warred with his instincts. He'd thought she was about to send him over, but he'd failed to use her title in his blurted response. Training a sub required consistency from the very start. Otherwise, there'd be confusion and misunderstandings, which would defeat the intended dynamics of their relationship.

Seconds ticked by, and then he finally inhaled deeply and let it out slowly. His gaze dropped to the floor. "I'm sorry. I meant to say, yes, Ma'am, I would like to come, please." His jaw was still rigid, but his words had been respectful.

"Very good. Failure to use my title or ask permission to speak unless I've asked a direct question will always be met with a negative response. Compliance will result in a positive one."

She resumed the hand job she'd been giving him and sped up the pace. Leaning forward, she licked one of his nipples and then the other. She could sense the strength and tension emanating from him. It wasn't long before he was nearing the crest of his climax. Her hand holding his balls felt when his body drew them inward. "Come for me, Michael."

As soon as the words were out of her mouth, she bit down on his nipple and tightened her hold on his cock. His body stiffened, and then, with a roar, his orgasm exploded. His eyelids slammed shut. Streams of semen shot from him, coating his abdomen and her hands. She continued to pump his shaft until he had nothing else to give her.

His body sagged as he leaned back on his heels again, gasping for air. "Holy—" He caught himself before it was too late. His eyelids lifted, and his gaze met hers. "P-Permission . . . to speak, Ma'am."

She gave him a pleased nod. "Permission granted."

"Holy shit . . . damn, that . . . was incredible."

Grinning, Charlotte released him and stood. "Stay there."

Before he arrived, she'd placed a bowl of water, a washcloth, and a towel on a table next to the room's loveseat. After wetting the washcloth and wringing out the excess, she returned to the sofa with it and the towel and began cleaning the evidence of her sub's release from his torso. He was still recovering, but his breathing was almost back to normal.

She reached over and grabbed his glass of water. "Drink the rest."

Once he was clean, she patted the cushion next to her. "Come up here."

Mike was a little wobbly on his feet, which was expected.

When he sat next to her, Charlotte took one of the couch's smaller throw pillows and put it in her lap. "Lie down and rest awhile."

His eyes narrowed again. "It feels weird that I got to come and you didn't."

"Don't worry, Michael. You'll have plenty of opportunities to give me orgasms. Just not tonight. This was all about you and seeing how much you trusted me and were willing to invest in a D/s relationship with me. Now, come lay down."

He hesitated a moment before following her command. Taking a blanket from the back of the couch, she laid it over him. For several minutes, neither spoke as she massaged his scalp and shoulders. The low jazz music became the only sound in the room. It wasn't long before sleep overtook Mike, and Charlotte smiled to herself.

My sweet, strong sub.

NINE

Sitting at a table in the pub between his mother and brother and across from his future brother-in-law, Mike tried to keep his mind on the subject—convincing his mother it was time for an assisted living facility. The one they wanted her to move into was only five or six minutes away from Mike's condo and only a little further away from the Trident Security compound where Jake and Nick's large apartment was located.

Mike had thought about moving back to his childhood home to help care for Emma, but he couldn't be there twenty-four hours a day and wasn't too keen on bringing in aides he didn't know to sit with her. As he and Jake had discussed, the assisted living facility would be best for many reasons. She'd be around people her own age, her medications would be monitored, and someone would be able to check on her at all hours.

They'd planned to have this discussion two days ago, but Ian had needed Jake and Nick to take care of a Trident case. But now, as Jake rattled off those valid reasons and a bunch of others of why the assisted living facility was a good idea,

Mike's mind kept wandering to Charlotte. He was still floored about the other night, how she'd made him come with more intensity than he'd ever experienced before and so quickly. Then he'd fallen asleep with his head in her lap. When he'd awakened about forty minutes later, they'd still been in the same position.

After asking him a few questions to determine his mental status, she'd gotten up and made omelets for them. While eating, they'd reviewed a D/s contract, with Charlotte filling in blanks as they negotiated and then agreed on different clauses. Mike had thought it would feel odd signing a sex contract, but it hadn't. It also hadn't just been about sex.

Sitting next to Mike at the table in her kitchen, Charlotte added a note in the margin of the contract, then glanced back up at him. Her eyes narrowed. "I can tell you want to ask me a question, Michael. Is something confusing or upsetting you?"

Chewing a mouthful of the delicious omelet, he tilted his head slightly from side to side, trying to get the words right in his mind before speaking them. He didn't want to sound like he was insulting her or being a chauvinistic ass. "I'm just not sure how this works outside of the bedroom or the club."

"You mean the dynamics of our relationship?"

"Yes."

Reaching over, she laid her hand on his arm. "Your submission isn't all or nothing here, Michael. In the bedroom and club, yes, I'll want . . . I'll demand your full submission. But that's where it ends. You're a strong, intelligent adult. Just like I don't want you to suppress your sexual submission, I don't want you to suppress who you really are outside of play, either. There, I want you to be my equal—side by side—give and take—neither one of us being the alpha or the omega. I'm not demanding you submit to me in other aspects of your life. And in the same respect, I won't stand for you trying to take over those aspects of my life. When we come across something where your knowledge or experience goes beyond mine, then yes, I'll let you take the lead. If it's something I excel in, then all I ask is that you give me the same courtesy. From there, we'll agree on how to proceed. Understood?"

HE'D FELT SO MUCH BETTER after she'd explained it to him. As they'd continued going through the contract, he'd felt more and more at ease with how the relationship would be. The end date of the contract was one month to the day they'd signed it, but Charlotte hadn't given him a definitive answer about whether or not they'd be renewing it at that point. And that was the only thing that was bothering him if he were being truthful with himself. Everything else seemed to . . . fit, he guessed was the word he was looking for. When he was in her arms, he felt like he was home.

She hadn't lied when she'd said there wouldn't be any sex between them the other night—or sex that involved her getting undressed and coming. Now, three days later, he was ready to beg her to let him see her again. They'd only spoken on the phone a few times since that night. That didn't mean the conversations hadn't been hotter than Hell.

Last night, as he laid in bed, naked at her command, she'd told him to describe what he wanted to do to her if she'd been there with him. It had been the most sensual phone sex he'd ever had in his life. Hell, it ranked up there with the best *sexual act* he'd ever had in his life. God help him when he finally got his cock inside her. He wasn't sure he'd survive.

"Mike? Hey, Earth to Mike."

He shook his mind clear and looked at his brother. "What?"

Jake rolled his eyes. "Want to stay in this conversation,

please? Can I have that stuff you got from the assisted living place about the cost breakdown?"

Shifting to the side, Mike reached back and pulled the folded papers from his back pocket. He handed them over to Jake as he addressed their mother. "I tallied up your social security check, your monthly pension from Southwestern Bell . . ." She'd worked in their customer service department for twenty years, starting in her late teens. It was where she'd met Sean Donovan and fallen in love with the Irishman. ". . . and the monthly dividends from the investments with your financial advisor, and all of that will cover about seventy-five percent of the bill each month at Twin Ponds. Your mortgage is low, so after we sell the house, plenty will be left over to cover the other twenty-five percent. And Jake and I will help if needed, but I don't think it'll come to that."

"It's not the money, dear," his mother said. "I don't want to give up my independence. And I have the house decorated the way I like it. It's my home."

"Mom, you won't be giving up anything—in fact, I think you'll have more freedom. Think of it this way—you won't have six huge rooms to dust and vacuum. There are two and a half baths in the house for one person. And none of your neighbors are around during the week. At Twin Ponds, there'll be plenty of people your age, and they have lots of great activities you can take part in. And Jake, Nick, and I will take you out whenever you want. We just want to make sure that while we're working, you'll have someone looking out for you."

"I don't know—"

"Emma," Nick interrupted, his tone soft for his future mother-in-law. "Why don't we take you over there to scope out the place before you decide? I haven't seen the inside, but the outside grounds look really nice. I think you'll like it." His gaze flitted past the older woman, and recognition kicked in. "Hey, Charlotte."

Mike's head whipped around, and his heart began to pound in his chest, the way it seemed to do every time the Domme was near nowadays. Her gaze met his, and he immediately began to recall the latest baseball stats—anything to keep from getting a hard-on while sitting next to his mother. Thank God the thought of the woman who'd given birth to him had the desired effect. At least he'd be able to stand and greet Charlotte without being embarrassed.

Just don't think about the phone sex, and you'll be fine. Damn it.

Climbing into her SUV, Charlotte tossed the file she'd been carrying onto the passenger seat. "Four down, one to go," she muttered as she turned the ignition key, and the engine roared to life.

Three mornings and one random evening a week, she made rounds to check on some of her parolees at their jobs or residences. Depending on the location and the ex-con's history, there were times she had an officer from Tampa P.D. accompany her on a visit. Today she'd only required backup on her first stop.

She suspected it was only a matter of time before low-life Simon McGee returned to his criminal ways and would probably put up a fight when she found evidence he was selling drugs once again. So far, if he was dealing, he wasn't sampling the product since his random drug tests had come up negative. And he either had a fantastic hiding spot at his mother's house, or the drugs were being held elsewhere.

Pulling out onto the highway, she headed for Donovan's Pub. She'd purposely made Jose Vega's check-in her last for the morning. She could then see if Mike was available for lunch before she returned to the office for her afternoon appointments. Suddenly, finding out if something could be between them long-term was important to her. For the first time since she'd entered the BDSM lifestyle, the thought of a contract's end date actually scared her.

What if he doesn't want to renew it at the end of the month? What if he isn't feeling the same things I am—things I've never felt before with any man?

It didn't take her long to reach her destination. At 11:30, there were already several vehicles parked in front of the pub. She knew the staff parked in a smaller lot behind the building—along with employees of the other shops in the strip mall—to leave more spaces available for patrons. To the right of Donovan's was a dry cleaner, a nail salon, and a Chinese takeout place. To the left was a small, owner-operated pharmacy that'd somehow survived after both a Walgreens and CVS had moved in nearby, a mixed martial arts studio, and on the far end, a convenience store. Through the large plate-glass windows of the studio, she could see a class of mostly women and a few men performing Tai Chi exercises.

Parking, she quickly found Jose's file among the others and exited the vehicle. The springtime sun shone high in the sky, but the temperature was still comfortable enough that she could wear a lightweight jacket to conceal the weapon on her hip. While she could open-carry with her shield visible on her belt, it tended to make some people nervous, so she usually hid it from view.

Striding into the pub, she paused momentarily to let her eyes adjust to the dimmer surroundings. A few tables were already occupied with people having lunch.

"Hi, Charlotte."

Turning toward the feminine voice, she spied Jenn

walking toward her. "Hi, Jenn. How are you?"

"Good. Sad and happy at the same time. I'm going to miss this place."

Charlotte smiled, giving the other woman a brief hug. "You've made some good friends here, and it's not like you'll never be in to visit."

"I know. Life goes on, right? Are you here to eat?"

"Actually, I'm looking for Mike and Jose. I need to speak with both of them." Jenn was fully aware of Charlotte's job and probably also knew Donovan's new sous chef had served time. While Mike was all for giving people a second chance, he also made sure his other employees were aware of who they were working with. During one of their recent evening chats on the phone, he'd mentioned to Charlotte it would be irresponsible of him not to. There was no guarantee the ex-cons wouldn't become repeat offenders. But he also stressed to his employees he wouldn't tolerate anyone harassing them or anyone else for things that belonged in the past. No one was perfect.

Jenn pointed to an occupied round table toward the back of the room. "Mike's over there with Mrs. D., Uncle Jake, and Nick, and you can go back to the kitchen to see Jose. He seems like a nice guy—I'm happy he's getting a second chance. He's got the cutest little five-year-old boy with his fiancée. I keep telling him he has to bring them by one day before I leave."

As Jenn hurried over to one of her customers who'd signaled for the check, Charlotte strode down the bar. Nick was the first one to spot her, and his grin grew wide. "Hey, Charlotte."

Mike's head whipped around to face her, and a combination of lust, shyness, and embarrassment filled his eyes. She was certain that the last emotion was there because of the elderly woman sitting to his right, with her back to the room.

It wasn't every day a male sub had to introduce his Domme to his mother.

From her seat, Mrs. Donovan glanced over her shoulder while all three men stood as Charlotte approached. Her gaze was drawn to the man who'd been occupying her thoughts lately—more than she'd expected him to. She loved the stain that appeared on his cheeks and knew he was recalling their phone sex from last night—it'd been incredibly hot. If Jake or Nick noticed Mike's reaction to her presence, neither acknowledged it.

"Hi, Charlotte," Jake and Mike said simultaneously.

"Hi." Her gaze moved to their mother. "Hello, Mrs. Donovan. How are you?"

The woman eyed Charlotte, and it was evident she didn't remember they'd met several times at get-togethers at the Trident compound, but she'd never be rude and say that. "Hello, dear. I'm fine, thank you for asking."

"Mom," Mike said, knowing his mother didn't recognize the other woman. "This is Charlotte. She's a friend of ours."

At that, Nick's eyebrow shot up, and a smirk appeared on his face, then disappeared just as quickly when Jake gave him the evil eye. It always amazed Charlotte how the men of Trident Security could have a whole conversation with each other without saying a word. It had to be a military thing because she'd never noticed it with those who'd never served.

"Oh, I remember." It was clear Mrs. Donovan didn't, but she was trying to cover to be polite. "Won't you join us, dear?"

Mike jumped at the suggestion and grabbed a chair from a nearby table. "Yes, have a seat. Are you hungry?"

"Actually, I am, but first, I need to talk to someone else."

"Uh . . . right . . . he's in the kitchen. I'll walk you back and order whatever you want while I'm there." He glanced down. "I'll be right back, Mom."

"Take your time. Jake and Nick will keep me company."

As Charlotte followed Mike toward the kitchen, she overheard Mrs. Donovan ask the other two men, "Is that Michael's girlfriend? She's very pretty."

Trying to ignore how good it felt to hear herself referred to as "Michael's girlfriend," Charlotte put on her professional face as Mike held open the swinging door to the kitchen for her. "What can I order for you?"

"I'd love the chicken salad sandwich—the one with the apples and cranberries. Thank you, Michael."

A blush appeared on his cheeks again. "You're welcome. Come back to the table when you're done, and I'll have Jenn bring your sandwich out."

As much as she wanted to step closer and kiss him, she wouldn't. This was his business, and she had her own duties to perform. But after that, maybe she could convince him to lock them in his office for a little while.

"Thank you," she repeated, giving him a brief heated stare before glancing around the large food prep area, not seeing who she was looking for.

Mike saw her confusion and addressed his chef. "Where's Jose?"

"Out back, taking a phone call." The big man hit a small silver bell with the spatula he was holding. "Daniella, order up."

When Mike started for the backdoor leading to the alley, Charlotte stopped him. "That's okay. I wanted to talk to him in private anyway."

"Sure . . . um . . . can I get you something to drink?"

"I'll take a Diet Coke with my lunch, thanks."

His gaze trailed down her body, stirring up her desire once more. "Diet Coke? Charlotte, the last thing you need is diet anything."

This time, it was her cheeks that heated—something that

rarely happened anymore. She shrugged. "I developed a taste for it back in college. The regular stuff is too sweet—I prefer something with a bite to it."

Winking, she turned on her heel and left him standing there, gaping at her.

The door to the alley was cracked open to let in some air, and Charlotte pushed it further. Sitting at a scarred, wooden picnic table some of the employees used for cigarette breaks, Jose's gaze darted to her when the door's hinges squeaked. His eyes went wide as he spoke into his cell phone. "Ah . . . look . . . I . . . uh, gotta go. My parole officer is here . . .yeah, later."

Disconnecting the call, he stood. "Um, hi, Ms. Roth. I . . . um . . . didn't expect you."

Striding over, she gestured for him to sit as she took the seat across from him, setting his file down on the table in front of her. "You weren't supposed to expect me, Jose. I'm sorry I interrupted your phone call."

Actually, she was curious about whomever he'd been talking to. His face had paled when he'd spotted her, and that, combined with his rush to end the call, piqued her interest. "I hope everything's all right." She glanced at his phone and then back to his face.

"Um . . . yeah, yeah, everything's fine. That . . . um . . . that was . . . my fiancée, Dina."

Between her training to become a parole officer and a Domme, Charlotte had gotten very adept at reading a person's body language and verbal responses. From how Jose's eyes shifted to the left before mentioning his fiancée, his stuttering, and how he squirmed in his seat, she was positive he was lying to her. But why he was lying was something she had to figure out.

Had he been talking to a girlfriend he had on the side that he didn't want anyone to know about? Or had he fallen back in with the wrong crowd? There could have been any other number of reasons he'd lied, but if she came right out and called him on it, he'd shut down completely. "How're she and your son doing?"

"They're ... um ... good, I guess."

She arched an eyebrow at him. "You guess? You mean you don't know?"

"No! I mean, they're fine. Dina and Tomas are just ... um ... visiting her parents for a few days, so I haven't ... haven't really seen them. But they're fine, really."

Her eyes narrowing, she leaned forward. "Jose, what's wrong? It's obvious you're upset about something. If you tell me, maybe I can help you."

He stood and started pacing with his hands shoved deep into the pockets of the white pants that were part of the cooking staff's uniforms. "Nothing's wrong. Dina and I ... we just got into an argument, that's all. She's staying with her parents for a few days while she cools off. Nothing's wrong, I swear."

Charlotte still didn't believe him, but when he wasn't more forthcoming with anything while she glared at him, she changed the subject. "Okay. Then how are things here at work?"

The tension eased from his shoulders as he sat back down. "Good. I like the job a lot. I've been on time every day. The people are ... um, really nice."

"That they are." She crossed her arms over her chest. "There's something you should know, Jose. I've known the owner and his family for several years now, so there'll be times you may see me here when I'm not working. I just wanted you to be aware of that and not think that I'm here watching you."

Surprise had flashed in his eyes when she said she knew Mike, but he nodded, his gaze darting everywhere but to her.

"Oh, okay. Thanks . . . thanks for . . . um . . . telling me. That's exactly what I would've . . . um . . . I would've thought. I'm staying straight, Ms. Roth. No worries there."

Uh-huh. Charlotte's bullshit meter was bopping into the red. Something was up with Jose, and she hoped she wouldn't have to lock his ass back up. The first thing she could do was check him for weapons. Then she'd demand a urine test. Great. Just what she wanted to do before lunch. "Empty your pockets for me, Jose."

His eyes widened briefly, but then he stood and started doing as he was told. He'd gone through this the first time she'd done a pop-by at the apartment he shared with Dina and Tomas. After tossing his wallet, a lighter, a half-empty pack of cigarettes, and a bus pass onto the table, he stepped back and let her look through the items. Charlotte examined and sniffed the cigarette package for signs of illegal drugs. Finding none, she went through his wallet—nothing out of the ordinary there.

Gesturing to the picnic table, she said, "Assume the position."

Placing his hands on the wood, he spread his legs. His head hung down between his shoulders as she patted him down from head to toe until she was satisfied he had nothing an ex-con wasn't allowed to have. "All right. You can take your things."

As he stuffed the items back into his pockets, she pulled a specimen cup in a sealed package from her purse. "Need a sample."

When she held it out, he took it from her and then gestured to the door. "There's a bathroom off the kitchen for the help."

She followed him inside and inspected every inch of the small room, including lifting the toilet's tank lid. Once she was sure there was no hidden bottle of piss or anything that would alter the drug test results, she stepped out to let Jose in with a few orders. "Don't flush or turn on the water. Leave the cup on the sink."

Charlotte shut the door and let him do his thing. It didn't take long, and when he came out, she reentered to test the sample in the little plastic cup. Pulling on a pair of latex gloves, she dipped the test strips into the urine one by one. There were twelve in all to detect marijuana, cocaine, ecstasy, amphetamines, methamphetamines, barbiturates, and six other categories of drugs.

After they all came back negative, she poured the last of the urine into the toilet and flushed it. Tossing the plastic cup and strips into the garbage, she turned to Jose, who was waiting outside the door. "All good. You can go back to work. I'll see you next Wednesday, right?"

"Yeah, Wednesday at nine a.m. Um . . . I just have to wash my hands." They changed places again, and after he was done, Jose nodded at her. "Thanks, Ms. Roth."

As she watched him hurry back to his workstation, she wasn't sure what he'd been thanking her for, but she sensed it was because she'd dropped the line of questioning he'd been uncomfortable with. Charlotte was torn between mentioning her suspicions to Mike without evidence that something was up with his employee and waiting until she had evidence. She'd hate to have Mike fire him based on a hunch.

After stewing over it for several moments, she decided to stay quiet for now. That didn't mean she was dropping it, though. Tomorrow or Friday, she'd do another drop-in at Jose's apartment—this time, with a uniformed officer in tow.

Picking up the file, she made a few notes, then slid it into her large purse. As she cut through the kitchen, she gave Jose a final glance before heading into the main restaurant. She found Mike and his family still sitting there. Charlotte's sandwich was on the table with a silver cover over it.

When Mike saw her approaching, he stood, pulled out the chair for her, removed the lid from her lunch, then hurried over to the bar and got her a fresh Diet Coke. Nick chuckled at the other man, and both Jake and Charlotte glared at him. Wisely, the younger man wiped the grin from his face and held up his hands in silent surrender.

Once he was sure Charlotte had everything she needed, Mike sat down beside her. While she ate, the conversation around the table resumed. From the sound of things, Mrs. Donovan was willing to see the assisted living facility, but she was still not convinced it was the place for her. "There's so much in the house. Where will it all go?"

Jake patted his mother's arm. "The apartments are a nice size, Mom. You can take the things that mean the most to you, and if there's not enough room for something, Nick and I or Mike will hold onto it for you. But there's a lot in that house you don't need anymore."

"But it'll take forever to go through everything." She frowned. "Maybe I should just stay in my house. I'm comfortable there. Charlotte, what do you think? Are your parents still in their own home?"

Startled, Charlotte grabbed her napkin and held it in front of her mouth while she chewed and swallowed the bite of the sandwich she'd just taken. "Um. Actually, Mrs. Donovan, my mom passed away a few years ago, and about six months ago, my dad moved into an assisted living facility near my sister in New Jersey, where I grew up. Like you, he was hesitant about it at first, but now that he's there, he loves it. There are plenty of people his age to talk to. The staff is really nice, and every time I talk to Dad, he's running off to participate in one activity or another.

"They have people who come in and do musical shows, teach yoga classes, and play games. He's in a cribbage club with a few people, and they play three afternoons per week.

Then at other times, the staff load everyone into a bus they have and take them out for a few hours for shopping or events. Dad really has a lot of fun. In fact . . ." she added with a twinkle in her eye, ". . . my sister and I think he's got a girlfriend there now, but he won't admit to it yet."

Mrs. Donovan grinned. "Well, good for him. Why shouldn't he have a girlfriend? We old people aren't dead yet. There's still a lot of hot romance left in these bones."

Wide-eyed, Nick, Jake, and Mike all coughed as if choking on their own tongues, to Charlotte's immense amusement. Emma waved her hand in the air and chastised her sons. "Oh, hush. I know no one ever wants to hear about their parents having sex, but how do you think I got pregnant with you two? Just because your father's dead doesn't mean I am. Maybe I will check out this place. I wouldn't mind a boyfriend who's still up for it."

As the Donovan boys had a combination of embarrassed-pink and appalled-green spread across their faces, Nick roared with laughter. "Way to go, Emma! Jake had a field day when Ian told me how he'd walked in on our folks going at it a few years ago. I'm so glad it was Ian and not me. I would've had to bleach my brain."

Charlotte winked at Mike, who shook his head in disbelief and chuckled. At least Mrs. Donovan was smiling again. Being part of a good, close family was something Charlotte knew well. However, with the physical distance between her and her dad and siblings, she missed feeling the comfort and sense of belonging that came with seeing them regularly. But as she sat there with Emma, Nick, Jake, and Mike, she felt as if she'd come home to where she belonged—and damn, if that didn't scare the crap out of her.

TEN

"All right." From the head of the long conference room table, Ian's gaze scanned the faces of his operatives. The Monday morning meeting had been to go over the current, recently completed, and new cases everyone was assigned to, even though a few people were missing. Lindsey Abbot, Val Mancini, and Darius Knight were still down in South America, working on a white-slavery case for the FBI. Doug Henderson, the head of Trident's Personal Protection Division, was over at Black Diamond Records coordinating things for country singer Summer Hayes's move from the California rehab hospital she was in, recovering from a car accident, to her home in nearby Indian Shores. The rest of the Alpha and Omega teams were in attendance. "Anyone else have anything to report or discuss?"

When no one spoke up, Jake stood. "Um, yeah. But it's off-the-job. Someone wants to talk to everyone. Hang on a sec."

Charlotte had called him last night and asked if she could speak to everyone following their meeting this morning. After finding out why, he'd agreed it was the best way to approach the situation. As if he didn't have enough shit on his mind. His mother's refusal to move into the assisted living, even after saying it was a nice place, drove him nuts. They would have to figure out a way to keep a better eye on her. Thank God Linda and Mike had managed to get Emma's car keys away from her. She still thought she'd misplaced them—both sets—and they'd turn up sooner or later.

Striding to the closed door, he opened it and called for Charlotte, who was waiting in his office across the hallway. She'd texted him during the meeting, letting him know she was there. After Charlotte entered the conference room, Jake closed the door again and returned to his seat. The parole officer was dressed in her usual work attire of comfortable dress pants, a button-down shirt, and low-heeled shoes. She'd already shed the lightweight jacket she'd been wearing to conceal her weapon, which was holstered on her hip. Attached to her belt, in front of the holster, was a round leather strap that her shield was pinned to.

"Good morning, gentlemen," she said with a smile. "I hope you don't mind my intrusion for a moment, but it's easier to have you all in the same room so I don't have to repeat what I have to say."

Ian raised an eyebrow in curiosity, as did a few others around the table. "No worries, Charlotte. What's wrong?"

Sitting next to Brody, she crossed her legs and sat back. "Who said anything was wrong?"

"Okay, then what's *not* wrong?"

Channeling her Domme persona, her gaze went around the table, landing on each man present before moving on to the next. "As Mistress China, I have an announcement to make and a request. Nick, since you already know what I'm going to say, you may remain in the room."

"Thank you, Ma'am," the youngest Sawyer responded with a grin. He was the only non-Dom in the room and had no problem with it. Several new members of Trident's Omega team had either already been Doms before coming to work for the company or were in the process of training to be one.

"I'll call Mitch later and speak to him about this too." Even though Mitch Sawyer was the club's manager, in addition to being co-owner, Ian held the title of Head Dom. With respect to that title, she turned to face him before tossing the little bomb on all of them. "I'll be bringing a new submissive to the club soon. Brody will have an easy time with his background check . . . considering it's Michael Donovan."

As Jake and Charlotte had both expected, jaws dropped around the table, and most gazes shot to Mike's brother. Jake held up his hand to ward off any questions. "I was surprised too, but after making sure this was what he really wanted to try, I promised to stay out of it. He's done the research and talked to Nick, so the decision is all his."

Brody chuckled. "The family that plays together stays together."

"The reason I wanted to tell you all in this setting . . ." Charlotte continued, ignoring the big geek's sarcasm, ". . . is I didn't want those looks on your faces when I bring him to the club next week. I'd appreciate it if you'd let your subbies know as well. Michael is nervous enough as it is. I know no one would intentionally make him uncomfortable, but I wanted to reduce the number of surprised expressions."

Ian nodded. "Okay, completely understood. Thanks for the heads-up. I'll pass the word around to a few others who'll recognize him."

"Thanks. I appreciate it. That's all I wanted to say. Short, simple, and to the point." Instead of getting up and leaving as Jake expected her to, she glanced at him. "Now, can I get a moment to talk to you alone about something else?"

"Sure."

As the meeting broke up, Charlotte and Jake stayed behind until everyone was gone. Standing, he moved and took the seat beside her. "What's up?"

Taking a deep breath, she let it out. She'd debated what to do since the pop-by she'd done for Jose and now hoped she was doing the right thing. "This is off the record."

"Okay."

"You know the new sous chef at the pub is one of my parolees." When he nodded, she continued. "I'm worried about him. I didn't think he'd be a repeat offender, and I'm not sure if that's what's going on, but something's up with him."

Jake frowned. "What did he do time for? Mike didn't tell me."

"Grand larceny of a vehicle. He was a chop shop supplier, but unlike most of those greedy little bastards, he thought it was the only way he could provide for his pregnant fiancée. You know the type—high school dropout and poor upbringing."

"Oh, yeah. You think he's fallen back on old habits?"

Crossing her arms, Charlotte shook her head. "That's just it—I don't honestly know. All I *do* know is when I did a pop-by at the pub yesterday, he wasn't the same guy who's been coming to my office over the past two months. Something was off—he wasn't thrilled to see me, even though he knew I'd be showing up there at some point. His drug test came up clean, didn't have any weapons on him . . ." She shrugged. "Nothing to give me a hint of what's going on. Usually, I let these things play out—I'm their parole officer, not their moral conscience—but this kid was really trying to put his past behind him. At least, I thought he was. He seemed to be trying to do right by his fiancée and kid. He'd even got his GED in prison."

"So, you want me to nose around a bit, on the q.t., to see if your instincts are dead on, as usual?"

"If you don't mind. I can't put my suspicions into his file—not without any evidence—and, truthfully, I want to help him before it's too late—*if* I can."

A smirk spread across Jake's face as his eyes lit up in amusement. "There's the other side of the Domme I know so well. Don't worry, I won't tell anyone you're an old softie under that Mistress China veneer."

Charlotte snorted softly. "That cat's already out of the bag. I know the subs call me 'Mother Hen' behind my back."

She'd said the nickname as if she abhorred it, but Jake knew better, and he barked out a laugh. "Ha! That they do. But you do know that's a compliment. It's one of the things that makes you a good Dominant." And she was—it was the main reason he'd come to his senses and agreed to stay out of her relationship with Mike. She was one of the best Dommes he'd ever known, including the one who'd trained him to be a Dom.

"Yeah, I know." She pulled a piece of paper from her purse and handed it to him. "Here's Jose's information."

After quickly scanning the data on the page, he folded it in half. "All right, I'll see what Nick and I can come up with—he loves playing private detective. I think for his next birthday, I'm going to get him a Sherlock Holmes hat, cape, and pipe."

"Kinky, Dr. Watson." Standing, she patted his shoulder. "Let me get back to work. I appreciate your help, Jake . . . and your support with Michael."

He stood and followed her to the door. "Just remember to keep his junk hidden when I'm around."

Mike watched as Mistress China paced back and forth in front of the class. Dressed in a skin-tight, black, spandex catsuit and thigh-high leather boots, she was sin on two legs. She'd asked him to join her this evening at the club even though it was closed on Tuesday nights. She was teaching a class with Master Stefan for new Doms and subs. While Mike couldn't play in the club until his physical was complete, Charlotte had said it would be good for him to see the place before it was filled with members scening all over.

There were eight couples in the class in the club's garden. The Dominants were lounging in comfortable chairs, facing the large section the instructors had roped off. The submissives were either resting on their Dom's laps or on pillows on the floor. Mike was sitting on a chair in the roped-off area. To his immediate right, Trident Security operative Logan Reese also sat in a chair. On his lap was his scantily-clad girlfriend, Dakota Swift, a Tampa police officer. Behind the three of them was a large St. Andrew's cross. Charlotte's demonstration tonight involved the whip, and Mike was thanking his lucky stars it wouldn't be his ass being lit up.

"So," the petite Domme was saying, ". . . as we have stated before, a Dom should never perform a scene with their sub that they haven't experienced for themselves."

A man, who'd been pissing Mike off by practically drooling over Charlotte, snorted obnoxiously, causing her to stop in front of him and cross her arms. "Problem, Master Roy?"

Mike didn't need to see her face to know she was glaring at the man, who shrugged in response. "There's no way I'm letting some chick whip me."

"Why's that? Because all women are beneath you?"

His eyes narrowed, but the stupid idiot didn't know when to keep his big mouth shut. "No. I'm just not some wimp who needs to be whipped by my mommy. And seriously, how hard is it to learn how to crack a whip?"

Whatever faint chatter there'd been among the other students ground to a halt as everyone stared at the ignorant bastard and the Domme, who was clearly trying to stop herself from kicking his ass out the door. Master Stefan rolled his eyes and shook his head in disgust but didn't interfere. Instead, he grabbed a straight-backed chair, spun it around, and straddled it, apparently settling in for the show that was about to start with Charlotte in the lead role.

Next to Mike, Reese groaned while Dakota whispered just loud enough for the two men to hear. "Somebody's gonna get it, and I'm so glad I get to watch."

Reese pinched his sub's thigh and reprimanded her in a low voice. "Quiet, subbie."

"Is that what you think of all the submissives in the lifestyle, Roy?" Charlotte asked the fool in front of her, and Mike noticed she'd dropped the title in front of his name. "That they're wimps?"

The man seemed to realize he'd fucked up and tried to backtrack. "That's not what I meant."

"If it wasn't what you meant, then why did it come out of your mouth?" She didn't wait for an answer. "I find most things verbalized are rarely unintentional. There's always a portion of truth or belief behind the words. Nick, come here, please."

Mike hadn't noticed his future brother-in-law standing in the doorway leading to the main club. Nick pushed off the door jamb he'd been leaning against and strode forward, his long, powerful legs easily eating up the distance. Several women and at least one male in the class, Dominants and subs, stared in unveiled interest at the good-looking man and his honed physique. He wore comfortable, faded jeans and a dark gray T-shirt that hugged his torso and showed off his bulging arms and chest.

Reaching the red velvet rope, he stopped, spread his feet shoulder-width apart, bowed his head, and clasped his forearms with his hands behind his back in a perfect presenting position. "Yes, Mistress China?"

She began to pace the length of the roped-off area again. "Nick, how long did your Dom train with a whip before he ever used it on a submissive?"

"From what Master Jake has told me, approximately eighteen months, Ma'am."

"And during those months, how often was he, himself, whipped?"

"Approximately once every week or two, Ma'am."

"And does he still occasionally get whipped by another Dominant?"

"Yes, Ma'am. Over fifteen years later, he still does."

"Before you moved back to Tampa, subbie, what was your profession?"

Mike could see the corners of Nick's mouth tick upward, even though his head was still bowed in respect, before he said, "I was a Navy SEAL, Ma'am. Hoo-yah!"

"Your Dom was also a Navy SEAL before entering the private sector several years ago, correct?"

"Yes, Ma'am."

"How often has your Dom whipped your back since you signed your original contract with him?"

"I lost count, Ma'am, but well over thirty times in the past two years."

"Do you enjoy being whipped?"

"Yes, Ma'am, very much."

"Why?"

"The subspace I hit during the scene is an incredible, drug-free high. It's also a way for Master Jake and I to bond further. I trust him completely, which pleases him—and the sex afterward is freaking amazing. We both benefit from it." The guy was obviously not embarrassed about anything he'd said, and Mike wished he was as confident as Nick was regarding the lifestyle.

"And has he ever broken your skin?"

"Not once, Ma'am."

"Has he ever whipped you in anger?"

"No, Ma'am."

"In frustration?"

"No, Ma'am."

"Under the influence of drugs or alcohol?"

He snorted as if it was a ridiculous question. "Absolutely not, Ma'am."

"Thank you, Nick. You're dismissed."

"Thank you, Ma'am." What the rest of the class didn't see was when Nick lifted his head, he gave Charlotte an amused wink before pivoting on his feet and returning to his spot in the doorway.

However, Charlotte wasn't done yet. Her rapid-fire questions reminded Mike of an attorney performing a cross-examination of a witness. "Master Logan, would you mind stating your prior profession?"

Reese appeared to have been expecting the question. "Not at all. I was in Special Forces in the military, but I can't specify further for security reasons."

"Special Forces are the best of the best in any branch, correct? And the training is grueling?"

"Absolutely."

"Have you ever been whipped, Master Logan?"

"You know I have since you and Mistress Roxy have been the ones wielding the whip during my sessions." Mike had only discovered earlier that Reese had been scening with the two Dommes. He'd been surprised, then realized there was so much he wasn't aware of when it came to Jake's teammates.

"I know you can't go into specifics, but why do you get whipped?"

"I find it therapeutic after experiencing a traumatic event during my time in the military that most people couldn't even imagine."

"Have I or Mistress Roxy ever broken your skin during a session?"

"Nope."

"How difficult is it to stay perfectly still during a whipping scene?"

"In the beginning, it was very difficult. It took weeks before I could trust you both enough to stand with my back to you and allow you to whip me."

"And now?"

He smiled. "Now, I trust you both 110%."

"What would happen if you moved while I was in mid-swing?"

"I'd risk throwing off your aim and velocity and would probably need stitches to close the deep laceration I'd end up with.

"Have you learned how to wield the whip?"

"Yes."

"Will you ever use the whip on your sub or anyone else?"

"Probably not," the Dom admitted. "Even after all these months of training, I wouldn't attempt it."

"Why?"

"Because I still slice through the practice paper. I can't . . . I won't risk doing that to my sub's skin or anyone else's."

"Thank you, Master Logan. Dakota, you've observed your Master's sessions with me for quite a while now, correct?"

The sub sat a little straighter in her Dom's arms. "Yes, Ma'am."

"Have you ever been whipped for a scene?"

Most, if not all, of the students were probably unaware Dakota had been attacked and whipped by the "Kink Killer," who'd been torturing and killing BDSM submissives several months ago, but Mike knew about it. How she'd recovered and then willingly let someone whip her for a scene blew Mike's mind. She was a helluva woman and cop.

"Yes, Ma'am. Two weeks ago, with Mistress Roxy. You and my Master were present."

"That was your first time?"

"Yes, Ma'am." Well, technically, it was since the other time hadn't been her choice.

"Why did you finally decide to be whipped after so many years in the lifestyle?"

Dakota's gaze softened as she looked into Reese's eyes. She smiled at him. "Because I love Master Logan and wanted to completely understand what he was experiencing. I know the reasoning behind his need to be whipped, and it meant a lot to me—and him—for me to experience it. I might not scene with a whip again—it's back on my hard limits because I'm not that big of a pain slut—but I can fully appreciate now what he's going through during a session."

"Master Logan, if you could use one word to describe your sub for scening with a whip, what would it be?"

The Dom was still staring at his sub with pure love in his eyes—it was as if no one else was in the room except the two of them. Reaching up, he cupped her cheek, and she nuzzled his palm. "Courageous. I know it was very hard for her to decide to try it. I'm proud of her."

Charlotte stopped pacing in front of the couple and smiled at Dakota. "So am I. Thank you both for sharing your experiences with the class."

She spun around, her fierce gaze finding that asshole, Roy, again. "If you haven't figured it out yet, 'wimp,' 'scaredy-cat,' 'momma's boy,' 'pansy,' and any other derogatory word or phrase out there are not what I—and most Doms—would *ever* use to describe our submissives. In fact, in my book, submissives are more courageous than any Dom could ever be. They're willing to face their fears and place their trust in a Dom's hand, and that's not something that should ever be done lightly. Master Stefan's submissive Cassandra, who couldn't be here tonight, puts her trust in him every time she lets him tie her up. There's so much that can go wrong during a Shibari or whipping scene—or any other scene for that matter—and the odds of something bad happening increase dramatically if the sub doesn't completely trust their Dom. So, Roy, if you think just calling yourself a Dominant means you're a good one, then you've got a lot to learn. Because your attitude is one I abhor to see in a so-called Dom."

"I agree," Master Stefan added. "You're here for all the wrong reasons, dude, and I strongly recommend your sub runs for her life—if you don't straighten your ass out—because you're a disaster waiting to happen."

Master Logan shifted Dakota on his lap. "I second that. Just because you *think* you've got the balls doesn't mean you do. You wouldn't last two seconds with a whip before screaming for your momma, boy."

Mike wasn't the only one stunned at the three Dominants calling Roy out in front of the rest of the class, but that didn't mean the fucker didn't deserve it.

Roy glared at Charlotte, but this time, he wisely kept his mouth shut. The tightness in his jaw said he was grinding his teeth, trying not to dig his grave any further. He also didn't look at the other two Doms.

Typical bully, Mike thought, *and a chauvinistic pig.* It was evident Roy still believed Charlotte, being the only woman, was the weakest of the three. Mike would disagree. His

Domme was the strongest person in the room, and he was damn proud of her.

Having made her point loud and clear, Charlotte turned and strode over to Mike. "Dakota, please stand. Master Logan and Michael, please remove your shirts and kneel."

As the three stood and began to do as requested, Charlotte addressed the rest of the class. "Since my submissive is not allowed to play in the club yet, and also has whipping on his hard-limit list, like most newbies to the lifestyle, I'll only be using him for warmup demonstration purposes. Dakota has been training with Mistress Roxy and me on how to prep her Master for a whipping scene. Her participation brings them closer together instead of alienating her for the scene's duration."

After removing his shirt, Reese knelt on a pillow that Dakota placed on the floor for him, with his back to the class. When she put another pillow next to the first, Mike thanked her and then lowered himself to his knees.

Standing next to Mike, Charlotte placed her hand on his shoulder and squeezed. "Just to be clear, this is not about imposing my dominance over another Master. It's about supporting and empowering others to practice the techniques safely and proficiently. Master Logan knows this and isn't intimidated by my request for him to be on his knees. The main reason they're on their knees for this part of the demonstration is if they were standing, they're both too tall for Dakota and me to properly prep them. If they were sitting, the chair backs would be in the way. I'll have to ask Master Mitch to order an ottoman or two for the garden.

"Masters, if there's a reason your subs cannot kneel for the prep, and you don't have a seat that doesn't limit your access, you can also have them lay down on their stomach. I don't recommend you have them stand during this part of the scene unless they're very experienced with it—they'll actually start to go into subspace once they've gotten used to it. Over time, your subs will also warm up faster to the prep, but you still need to ensure it's done properly. Don't rush it.

"Now, the first thing we'll do is joint compressions. Using the heels of our hands, we press down into the joints of their shoulders and massage their upper arms and back. It helps them clear their mind and allows the muscles to relax."

Mike's head hung down between his shoulders as Charlotte continued to explain what she was doing and why. Her hands worked him over, and he relaxed further and further into her touch. He tuned everyone out as her voice vibrated through him. It'd finally struck him during her speech earlier to that asshole—Charlotte wasn't with Mike because she thought he was weak—she wanted him because she saw his strengths.

Jake had never brought anyone he'd been dating to meet Mike and their mother before Nick. Mike realized now it wasn't because he'd been embarrassed or ashamed of who he was seeing but because none of them had been good enough. Jake wasn't with Nick because he thought his sub was beneath him. Instead, he'd fallen in love with the man he thought was his equal or better.

Charlotte's dominant nature didn't mean she wanted someone who was spineless and feeble. She wanted a sub who would challenge her—someone who was secure enough in himself to trust her implicitly.

Was he that man? Mike wasn't sure. Did he want to be that man? *Damn fucking straight.*

Eleven

"You're awfully quiet, Michael. Did the demonstration freak you out?" Charlotte could usually read his facial expressions and body language, but as they walked through the club, she wasn't sure what was going through his mind.

He glanced at her and shook his head. "No, actually, it didn't—and that surprises me. I'm still not sure I could stand there and let you whip me, but it was amazing to watch. How long did it take you to learn how to do that without breaking the skin? Logan mentioned practice paper."

"Mm-hmm. You tape a piece of paper to a wall or a cross, and that simulates the sub's skin. If it tears, you've injured your sub. As for how long it took for me to be able to get through a whole scene without ripping the paper, it was a little longer than eighteen months. I will confess that the first time I whipped a live person—who happened to be my instructor—I was so nervous I almost threw up beforehand. But I managed to get through the scene without sending him to the emergency room. I still practice with paper a few times a week. It's one of those things that if you don't keep up your skills, they'll fail."

They passed by the bar area. While it was closed, two couples were standing there, chatting with the club's co-owner Mitch Sawyer and Travis "Tiny" Daultry, who was the head of security for the club and the Trident compound. Some of the students had stayed behind to watch two of Stefan's Shibari Masters-in-training practice their techniques.

It had been almost an hour since Logan had hit subspace after Charlotte had taken the whip to his back. She'd expertly left dozens of red welts on his skin before his knees had given out. Stefan and Dakota had helped her release Logan's restraints and move him onto a bed in one of the garden's cabanas. Dakota had applied Arnica gel to each stripe on her Dom's back while Charlotte had monitored his breathing and mental status. Once she was convinced he was stable and the only thing he needed to complete his aftercare was rest, she'd left him with Dakota, sound asleep.

Usually, Charlotte would monitor a person she'd whipped longer, but Stefan had assured her he'd remain nearby in the garden in case Dakota needed him. He wouldn't be more than a few feet from the cabana while observing his students. Once Logan woke up, Dakota would then drive him home.

When they reached the lobby door, Mike held it open for Charlotte and then followed her outside. They'd planned to stop by the pub for dinner, so Mike could also check in with his staff. "Well, I hadn't expected to find it as fascinating as I did. I don't know if that had anything to do with the beautiful Domme cracking the whip, but I'm pretty sure it did."

A smile spread across her face at his flirtation. It would take him a while to relax into their relationship, but his teasing told her he was becoming more comfortable with her. "Why, thank you, Michael."

"You're welcome, Ma'am," he responded with a grin. He

pushed open the door leading to the outside stairs above the parking lot and, again, let her walk through first—the perfect gentleman.

They were almost to the bottom of the stairs when angry shouting caught their attention. Charlotte scanned the vehicles in the parking lot until she spotted the source. Master Roy had his submissive by the upper arm and was cursing at her as he dragged her toward his truck.

"Let go of me!" Susan screamed, fighting to get loose. Her free hand swung at him, and she tried to kick him, but the five-foot-nothing woman was at a huge disadvantage against the six-foot man. "You're hurting me!"

"Get the fuck in the truck! We're outta here."

Before Charlotte could do or say anything, Mike was sprinting across the parking lot. She took off after him, glancing around.

Damn it! Where are the guards when you need them?

She didn't doubt Mike could handle himself if it came to fisticuffs, but if Roy had a weapon on him, Charlotte wasn't sure what would happen. The compound's guard shack had been moved closer to the main road after the fence line had been extended outward to keep the media and lookie-loos from getting pictures of the club members. A vindictive ex of two Masters had violated The Covenant's non-disclosure agreement and had paid for it in several lawsuits. And after the Trident guys and their significant others had ended up as targets for one reason or another over the past two years, Ian and Devon had beefed up their security measures even further. Armed guards were roaming the compound, and several dogs were in training to work with them. But the compound had also doubled in size as the Sawyers continued to buy up the acreage surrounding it.

When Mike reached the couple, he got between them and shoved Roy back, forcing the bastard to break his hold on

Susan. Then, so Roy couldn't reach for her again, Mike tucked her behind him. "What the hell do you think you're doing?"

"Back off, subbie," Roy said with a snarl, stressing the last word like it was something that repulsed him. "This is none of your fucking business!"

Charlotte reached the trio and grabbed Susan's shoulders, pulling her farther away. If the two men started exchanging blows, she didn't want the woman to get hurt.

With his fists clenched at his side, Mike took a step forward. "I'm making it my business, jackass! I hate dirtbags who abuse women!"

Rage flared in Roy's eyes, and he took a swing at him, but Mike was faster. Dodging right, he avoided the punch before unleashing one of his own, connecting with the other man's cheek. Roy went down like a fallen tree, twisting and landing face down as Charlotte heard footsteps rapidly approaching. Glancing over her shoulder, she saw Mitch and Tiny running toward them, with Master Wayne and his sub, Nancy, on their heels. The club owner and head of security both slid to a halt and stared in amusement at the aftermath of the one-two match.

Tiny barked out a laugh. "Damn, Mike, nice right jab. I'm gonna tell Jake to stop taking it easy on you when you spar with him."

Shaking his bruised hand, Mike snorted. "Don't you dare—not until I get a chance to catch him off guard. Shit, that hurt." He turned toward the others, his gaze seeking out Susan. Seeing her rubbing her bruised arm, he asked, "Are you okay?"

The dark-haired woman nodded. "Y-yeah, thanks. I didn't realize what an asshole he was until today. I told him I wanted out of our contract, and that's when he grabbed me and started yelling. I might be a submissive, but I'll be damned if I let any guy abuse me."

Charlotte's arm was still around Susan's shoulder in comfort, but it was clear the sub would be okay—she had spunk. Giving her a final squeeze, Charlotte released her.

Her anger ebbing but still present, the Domme's annoyed gaze met Wayne's, and the man raised his hands in self-defense. "Don't look at me. I didn't like the guy from the start. The only reason I said more than two words to him was because Nancy and Susan are best friends."

"It's true," Susan confirmed. "We met Roy at a munch. He said he was experienced in the lifestyle and offered to introduce me to it. He was nice at first, but I know now it was all a front."

From where he lay on the ground, Roy groaned. Standing over the semi-conscious man, Mitch glanced at Wayne. "Can you drive Susan home, please? Roy will be on his way after he understands he's never to contact her again. I'll also make sure he's banned from every lifestyle club within a hundred-mile radius."

There was no doubt Mitch would make that happen. He and his two cousins were some of the most responsible Doms Charlotte had ever known. They despised people who hid behind the veil of the BDSM community as an excuse to abuse others just as much as she did. When they'd first opened The Covenant several years ago, they'd instituted a network for the club owners and managers to be able to pass on information to each other easily.

It'd started with the Tampa Bay-area lifestyle establishments, but word had spread, and the owners and managers around the country had expressed a desire to be a part of it. There was a rather long list of people who'd been banned for one reason or another, and Mitch always followed up with new entries to ensure there was a valid reason for the expulsion. The members of the BDSM community tended to be close-knit and valued their privacy and safety. It grated on most Doms if a sub was harmed in any way, even if they didn't know them. The Dominants of the community tended to feel the need to protect them all.

"Susan," Mitch continued. "Since Master Wayne and Nancy have applied for membership here, if you'd still like to explore the lifestyle, I can pair you up with one of our single Doms for training. I'll help you negotiate a contract to include or exclude anything you want. You'll have to go through the club's vetting process like everyone else, but once that's done, you can play."

Her eyes widened in surprise. "Um . . . thanks, Master Mitch, but I couldn't afford the membership fees here and—"

He raised his hand and cut her off. "We can work something out, little one. We have several subs who work off most of their membership fees by waiting tables, cleaning, or working in the shop. And we'll be putting in a child-care area soon, so we'll be looking to fill some positions there too. Again, it's up to you." He pulled his wallet from his back pocket and handed her a business card. "Think about it and call me if your answer is yes or if you want to discuss it further."

"Thank you, Master Mitch. I appreciate it." Holding the card, Susan glanced down and realized she was missing something. "Um, my purse is in Roy's truck. He's got the keys in his front right pocket, I think."

Tiny unceremoniously rolled Roy onto his back and fished into his pocket. Pulling out the keys, he hit the button to unlock the doors of the nearby vehicle. Susan quickly retrieved her purse, then slammed the passenger door shut again with a little more force than necessary, causing Charlotte to grin. As the sub was about to pass by Mike, she stopped and put her hand on his arm. "Thank you again." Going up on her tiptoes, she gave him a peck on the cheek.

A blush bloomed across his face. "You're welcome. Stay safe."

"I will." After one last look of disgust in Roy's direction, she left with Wayne and Nancy.

Tiny looked at Mitch. "What do you want me to do with him?"

Glancing at the injured man, who was slowly coming around, the club owner seemed to think it over for a moment before answering. "Unfortunately, what I *want* to do with him differs from what we *should* do with him—let's get his ass up and have a little chat."

Striding over to his own vehicle, Mitch unlocked the trunk and retrieved several sixteen-ounce bottles of water. He tossed one to Tiny, and the two of them opened the bottles and poured them onto Roy's face. The man sat up, groaning and sputtering. "What? What the fuck! Knock it off!"

Reaching down, Tiny grabbed him by the front of his wet shirt and hauled his ass up—an easy feat for the six-foot-eight, former professional football player. When Roy tried to free himself, Tiny growled, which caused the shorter man's eyes to go wide and the rest of his body to freeze as if he suddenly realized he was in deep shit. Tiny got right in Roy's face and laid out the facts. "You're not going anywhere until we have a little chat. Your only other option is I tie you to a cross and let Mistress China whip your ass—I'm sure she'll take that offer in a heartbeat. Now, unless you want to lose a few layers of skin, I suggest you and I take a little walk. I think someone needs to educate you about how to treat a lady, and I'm volunteering to be your teacher."

Charlotte did her best to keep a glare in place—instead of laughing out loud—when a panicked expression spread across Roy's face, and the color drained from his cheeks at Tiny's not-so-subtle threat. After a moment, he nodded, and Tiny led him away from the remaining group, his big paw of a hand tightly gripping the other man's shoulder. Mitch called out after them, "Just don't feed him to B.D.S.M., big guy! You know Kat has them on a strict diet!"

The protection dogs Boomer's wife, Kat, was training for the compound had been dubbed B.D.S.M. by Ian—Bravo, Delta, Sierra, and Mike, using the military radio alphabet. Charlotte knew *her* Mike had gotten a chuckle out of hearing there was a kick-ass German Shepard with his name.

With his unoccupied hand, Tiny waved over his shoulder as he explained the rules of good etiquette, and the result of breaking those rules, to Roy.

Confident everything would be taken care of, Charlotte and Mike said goodbye to Mitch before walking over to Mike's vehicle. He opened the passenger door for her and, after she climbed in, shut it and strode around to the driver's side. After he settled into his seat, he started the engine and turned on the AC to cool off the interior. But then his hand froze on the gear shift as he stared out the windshield. "Are you mad at me?"

Startled by his question and the nervous way it was spoken, Charlotte shifted in her seat to face him and studied the hard set of his jaw. She wasn't sure where he'd gotten the idea she was mad at him and needed to set things straight immediately. "Michael, look at me, please."

Swallowing hard, he turned his head. Charlotte reached up and cupped his cheek. "Mad is the last thing I feel right now. I'm proud of you for rescuing Susan, and I know punching Roy was necessary after he swung at you. I didn't expect anything less from you. Yes, I'm not a fan of violence, but I'm also aware that sometimes it's unavoidable."

The tension left his jaw and shoulders. Grinning, she

trailed her hand down his face, neck, chest, and lower, her gaze never leaving his eyes. The uncertainty she saw there was replaced with lust as her hand drifted over his groin. "If anything, seeing you going all Rocky Balboa on him kinda makes me want to jump your bones. Are you okay with ordering takeout?"

Throwing the shifter in gear, he winked at her. "Takeout? To hell with that. Delivery's better. Your place or mine, Mistress?"

Twelve

Charlotte's heart was pounding as she led Mike to her bedroom, and it hadn't been from the red light he'd almost missed getting them back to her house. No, not at all. Instead, it had everything to do with the man himself. Somewhere along the line, he'd come to mean a lot more to her than just her sub or a temporary distraction.

When they'd sat down and negotiated their contract, she'd made it very clear she was giving him an opportunity to explore his sexual submissiveness. They wouldn't be "dating," although they'd spend non-playtime together. She'd told Mike she intended to use that time to educate him further and would eventually be letting him go at the end of their contract—or maybe after the end of a second renewed contract.

But now, the thought of an end date for this—whatever this was growing between them—was becoming unbearable. Maybe it was because they'd known each other for a while before taking that step into a D/s relationship. While before her birthday, she wouldn't have classified them as friends, he'd been more than just an acquaintance to her. Hell, she didn't know what they'd been before this, but now, for the first time since college, she wanted something more than a simple D/s relationship with no deep emotional attachments involved.

Stopping at the end of her bed, she faced him. "Strip, Michael. I want to see all of you." Especially that erection bulging in his pants. "Then stand in a presenting position."

Charlotte's gaze roamed his body as he removed each article of clothing. Once he was gloriously naked and his clothes were neatly folded on the hope chest at the foot of her bed, he stood before her. His hands were behind his back, clasping the opposite forearms, and his feet were shoulder-width apart. Moving forward, Charlotte ran her hands up his chest and down his upper arms. They skimmed over his abdomen, and his cock responded to her touch by twitching and bobbing as if beckoning her to wrap her hands around him. Going up on her toes, she placed several kisses along his jaw. Lust flared in his eyes as he silently watched her, his breathing and the pulse in his neck increasing.

Stepping back, Charlotte picked up a lighter from her dresser and set several candles around the room aflame. She then stood before him and held her arms out. "Undress me, Michael."

From his surprised expression, one would think he'd just won the lottery. Instead of walking behind her to undo the zipper that ran down her back, he slowly reached around her and found the small pull tab. Inch by inch, he lowered it, garnering a smile from her. He wasn't rushing, and that pleased her. It was as if he were unwrapping a Christmas present, savoring every moment.

Once the zipper stopped at her lower back, he peeled the two halves of the stretchy material from her shoulders and down her arms. She hadn't been wearing a bra—her perky 34B breasts allowed her to get away without one when she felt like it—and Mike's breath hitched as he uncovered her. Charlotte had banished any and all ill-conceived self-doubts about her body after her first year in the lifestyle.

Men and women came in all shapes and sizes. What one person loved in people they were attracted to differed from the next. Just because a woman's breasts were too small or her ass was too big, based on the fashion industry's and Hollywood's unrealistic dimensions for what women should look like, didn't mean every man out there felt the same way. The first step in gaining the confidence to walk around half or completely naked in a club was to love and be comfortable in your own body.

When Charlotte had been training under another Domme, Mistress Petra had instructed her apprentice to write a list of what she considered her physical flaws. Then without revealing that list to anyone, Petra had taken Charlotte around a club, randomly approaching Doms and subs and asking them what they thought Charlotte's best physical features were and what was the first thing they noticed and found attractive about her.

To the Domme-in-training's surprise, what she'd thought were her worst features were what others had claimed to be her best. Since then, she'd learned to love every inch of her body and appreciate others no matter what size or shape they were. As the cliché goes, beauty is only skin deep. But what glows brighter than any physical beauty is what's in a person's heart. It was one of the reasons most Doms despised hearing any submissive put themselves down for any self-perceived flaws.

Dropping to his knees, Mike unzipped one of her boots and then the other. Using his shoulders for support, she lifted her right foot, allowing him to remove the boot before switching to the other one. Grabbing the material that was now bunched at her waist, he slowly drew it down her body.

"Jesus," he whispered when he caught sight of her unadorned pussy. Taking a deep breath, he inhaled her scent and groaned. "So damn beautiful." His voice was so low that she'd almost missed the compliment.

Leaning on his shoulders again, she stepped out of the catsuit. "Please fold that and place it next to your clothing, Michael."

"Yes, Mistress."

He neatly folded the garment and set it on the hope chest before returning to her again. His heated gaze warmed her skin. Her nipples pebbled, and her pussy wept. She closed the distance between them. Taking his hands, she brought them to her breasts. "Touch them, Michael. Use your hands and your mouth."

Surprising her, he dropped to his knees. Without her heels on, she was much shorter than he was, and kneeling brought his mouth almost to the same height as her chest. Her lover cupped the small orbs, feeling their weight. He massaged her flesh before leaning forward and taking one stiff peak into his mouth. An electric current shot through Charlotte, causing her to gasp as all her nerves, from head to toe, seemed to rejoice at once. Her head fell back, and she moaned as she delved her hands into Mike's hair, holding him to her. His tongue flicked over her nipple before he sucked on it. She felt the suction all the way in her core. Switching over to the other breast, Mike gave it the same attention, spiking her desire.

With a pop, he released the suction on her tit and lifted his gaze to her face. His eyes were filled with lust . . . and something more—something Charlotte couldn't bring herself to analyze at the moment. "Mistress. please, I want . . . no, I need to make you come. I need to watch you shatter more than I need my next breath. Please tell me how to do that."

Charlotte's heart swelled. This was what she loved about D/s relationships—the power exchange—the give and take—, but this time, it felt like so much more. What she felt for Mike was far beyond anything she'd ever felt for a man. She was in deep but had to give him time. It was possible the awe and curiosity he was experiencing as a first-time sub would fade, and he'd be all too willing to end the contract when the time came. But she'd deal with that later. For now, she'd show him how much she wanted him.

Cupping Mike's cheek, she smiled. "Stand, my beautiful sub."

A blush passed over his face, but he wisely didn't challenge her use of the word "beautiful." When he got to his feet, she took his hand and led him around to the side of the bed. She climbed onto the mattress, pulling him with her until he was draped across half her body. His cock was hard and heavy against her hip. She stared into his eyes. "I want you, Michael. Kiss me."

He slowly lowered his head until their lips met. At first, it was a gentle kiss, but as seconds passed, she encouraged him to be bolder. Opening her mouth, she nibbled on his lip. His tongue darted out and dueled with hers.

Taking his hand, Charlotte trailed it down her torso and hissed when his finger brushed against her clit. She felt the tension in his hand and knew he was waiting for her to tell him what she wanted. Using her own finger, she pushed his into her slit and moaned as her body yielded to him. Her finger joined his inside her and set the pace she craved.

Breaking the kiss, Charlotte brushed her lips across his jaw. "I want your mouth on my pussy, sweet Michael. "

Lifting his head, his gaze met hers. "I want that, too, Mistress."

She removed her finger from her core and brought it up to his mouth. "Taste."

Opening wide, he wrapped his lips around the digit and sucked it into his mouth. His tongue swirled around it, licking her juices. He moaned as his eyelids fluttered shut. When he shifted lower on the bed, she pulled her finger from his mouth and pointed to the side of her neck. "Kiss me here."

He followed her order, placing a soft, sweet kiss on her skin.

Charlotte lowered her hand and pointed to the top swell of her breast. "And here."

Again, Mike did as he was told, but this time he added a little tongue lick. Meanwhile, his finger continued to fuck her pussy at a leisurely pace. Charlotte clenched her walls around him, trying to maintain her self-restraint. But for the first time in God knew how many years, she was very close to losing control. She'd always heard sex with the right person took it to a whole new level—one that changed all the rules—and right now, with this man, she had a feeling that was about to happen.

"And here." Her finger was now between her breasts.

Slowly, she mapped out a trail down her torso as Mike followed her verbal breadcrumbs. When her hand reached her mound, she spread her first two fingers, making a "V" just above her clit. "And here."

He placed a light kiss on her clit, followed by a lick, and Charlotte almost catapulted off the bed. "Oh, yes! Michael, eat me!"

Instead of attacking her with his mouth as she expected, Mike took his time, licking and sucking on her clit, driving her higher and higher. His finger continued to plunge in and out of her vagina. Charlotte's hips undulated under his touch. Her breathing and moaning increased with every pass of his tongue. She was getting close, but she needed more—more than just her own pleasure.

Grabbing his hair, she pulled his mouth off her. His gaze cut to her face as she clenched her thighs together, stilling his hand. "Get a condom from the nightstand drawer, Michael, and give it to me. The first time you make me come, I want you to go over the edge with me."

Desire raged in his eyes. Sitting up, he opened the top drawer of her nightstand. She saw his shoulders relax when he realized it was a new, unopened box. She'd actually gotten it the day after her birthday—it had been a very long time since she'd invited a man into her private sanctuary, preferring to play in the club. Her home was where she could sit back, kick off her shoes, remove her bra, and be a homebody with a pint of mint chocolate chip Häagen-Dazs.

She had no desire to be a twenty-four-hour Dominant. There was too much stress and responsibility involved. Instead, she'd preferred to keep her three lives—a Domme, a parole officer, and an occasional introvert—separate. But with Mike, she found those three worlds merging, and she no longer tried to stop them.

Handing her a condom, Mike knelt between her legs as she sat up and ripped open the small foil package. She placed the latex disk on the tip of his full erection and slowly unrolled it down to the root of his cock. He twitched in her hands and groaned loudly at her touch. Lying back down, Charlotte set her feet flat on the mattress and crooked her finger at Mike. Reaching down, she spread her labia apart. "I want you inside me."

Grabbing his cock, Mike tilted it toward her slit as he held himself above her with a hand next to her shoulder. His eyes never left hers as the tip of his shaft speared into her, one excruciatingly slow inch at a time. Her walls quivered and stretched as they accepted him. When he was buried to the hilt, she wrapped her legs around his waist. Her feet dug into his ass every time he thrust deep. The friction quickly brought her back to the peak of the sexual mountain she'd climbed just moments before.

Charlotte wedged her hand between their bodies. The heel of her hand pressed down on her clit while she V-ed her fingers again on either side of his cock, extending the grip her vagina had on him. Her legs around him urged him to pump faster.

"God, woman, I'm not going to last long. You feel so fucking incredible," he said with a gasp, and Charlotte was too close to nirvana to reprimand him for not using her title.

"I'm not going to last either." Her walls closed tightly around him. Her mind had gone blank to everything but the pleasure he was giving her. When she knew the inevitable was near, she scored his back with her fingernails. "Come with me, Michael. Oh, God, yes! Come with me now!"

Her lover made one final thrust, and his body stilled as his orgasm overtook him. His release set off her own, and they both screamed each other's name. Though Mike's eyelids had slammed shut at the moment of impact, Charlotte had forced hers to stay open. He gave her everything he had, and she did the same in return.

As their climaxes faded, the tension in his muscles began to ease. He collapsed on top of her, and she willingly took his weight, even as she felt him rest most of it on his forearms which were on either side of her head. She reveled in the cocoon of his body as their lungs heaved for oxygen.

Charlotte couldn't remember a time she'd orgasmed as hard as she just had, and she had a feeling it wouldn't be an isolated occurrence with Mike. He was still inside her, and she wanted him to stay there as long as possible—it was where he belonged.

Thirteen

Charlotte laid her head on Mike's shoulder as he cuddled her closer to his side. Absentmindedly, he stroked her bare back with his fingers. She returned the favor by making small, sensual circles with her hand over his chest. He let the silence hang in the air for a few moments, working up the courage to ask her the question that had been on the tip of his tongue for the past week.

"You're thinking too much, Michael." Her warm breath caressed his neck as she spoke. "What's on your mind?"

It still surprised him how in tune she seemed to be regarding his moods or emotions. "Can I ask you something?"

Rising on her forearm, she looked him in the eye. "Don't ever feel you need my permission to ask me anything if we're not scening. If I can answer it, I will. Maybe not right away, but never be afraid to ask." She returned to her original position. "Now, what's your question?"

Mike opened and closed his mouth twice before the words finally came out. "Why are you in the lifestyle? What do you get out of it? I read that many people are just wired that way, but I get the feeling it's a lot more than that for you. Something happened in your past that made you seek it out, didn't it?"

Seconds ticked by, and he thought she wasn't going to answer. Her fingers had started making those lazy swirls in his chest hair again. "You're the first submissive who's ever asked me that."

She turned her head slightly and kissed his collarbone before resting her head on his shoulder again. "Growing up, I lived in this great neighborhood in New Jersey. We were close enough to New York City to experience all the fun stuff to do there but far enough into the suburbs that we could play in the street without worrying about traffic and stay out after dark as long as it wasn't a school night. We had block parties every summer, and in the winter, there was a pond between our backyard and a park that would freeze over for ice skating. It was very idyllic. At least, it was for a while. Everything was great until my thirteenth birthday."

She paused, and after several long moments, he asked, "What happened on your thirteenth birthday?"

"Everything changed." She hesitated again before continuing. It was the first time he'd ever heard her sound less than confident. "Maggie O'Connor had been my best friend since we were about five years old. She lived six houses down, and you could always find us at either her house or mine. Our moms were good friends—they were both nurses in the maternity ward at the local hospital on the three to eleven p.m. shift. Her father was a dispatcher for the police department and worked mostly overnights, so he wasn't around much during the day unless he had the night off.

"When we started junior high school, I didn't see Maggie as much because we were in different classes. I was kind of hurt, thinking she was avoiding me or leaving me out of things. My mom tried to explain that as kids get older and their circle of friends widens, sometimes they grow apart from the ones they'd been close to. Maggie and I still saw each other, but she'd changed—she was quieter, didn't want to do things we'd always done, stuff like that.

"For my thirteenth birthday, Mom suggested I have a slumber party that Saturday night and invite Maggie and a bunch of my other friends, new and old, so they could all get to know one another better. The night of my party, we had everything all set up in the finished basement of my house—snacks, movies, music, and games. My dad took my brothers out for dinner and a movie so they wouldn't bother us.

"Around eight o'clock, I noticed Maggie still wasn't there. My mom called their house, and Maggie's dad said she wasn't feeling well and wasn't coming to the party. I remember being so pissed at her, and when a few of the other girls started being stuck-up bitches and making fun of her, I joined in." Charlotte took a shuddering breath and let it out slowly. "It wasn't my finest hour."

Her fingers had stopped moving at some point and now rested flat over his sternum. Mike brought his free hand up and set it atop hers, amazed at how much smaller it was than his own. One would think her petite stature would mean she was fragile, but instead, she was the complete opposite—and damn if that didn't turn him on for some obscure reason. "Most kids are like that at that age."

"I know—peer pressure and puberty are a crappy combination. Still doesn't make it any easier to remember how selfish and bitchy I was then. Anyway, I didn't see Maggie on Sunday. She didn't call me, and I was still pissed, so I didn't call her. The next day, she wasn't at the bus stop, and I started to think that maybe she really was sick. Then, in the middle of fourth period, I got called to the principal's office. My mom and dad were there with two detectives."

"Shit," Mike murmured into her hair. He could only

imagine what the rest of the story was, but there was no way it would be good.

Charlotte let out a sad, little snort. "Exactly. They asked me all sorts of questions about Maggie, wanting to know if she'd told me any secrets over those last few months. It turned out her bastard father had started molesting her about five or six months earlier. The last time was the day after my birthday party. Her mom had taken an overtime shift at the hospital. When she got home just after eleven p.m., Maggie was in her bedroom, presumably asleep, and her husband left for his midnight shift at work as if nothing had happened.

"When Mrs. O'Connor got up the next morning, she thought Maggie had already gone to school, but later, when she went to put away some laundry, she found Maggie had hanged herself in the bedroom closet during the night. Mrs. O'Connor called 9-1-1, and a bunch of the cops and detectives arrived at the house—one of them had driven the bastard home because he was putting on this act that he was shocked his daughter had committed suicide. In reality, he was probably worried they would find out he'd been raping her. When one of the detectives found a note Maggie had left, apologizing to her mother and detailing what her father had been doing to her, he confronted the bastard. O'Connor knew he was fucked, pulled out a gun, and shot himself in the head before anyone could react."

Pushing herself up into a sitting position, she swung her leg over his torso and straddled his hips, her pussy hot against his swelling cock. Damn, he'd never get enough of her. He rested his hands on her knees, knowing waiting for her to give him an order would be worth it—the anticipation of not knowing what was coming next or when was a helluva turn-on.

Leaning down, she brushed her lips across his. "So, that's

my sordid story. The one that helped mold me into the woman I am today. After I'd learned why Maggie had killed herself, I swore no man would ever touch me without my consent."

She rocked her pelvis against his, causing him to groan and his eyes to roll back in his head for a moment. "Maybe it was a combination of nature, nurture, and experience, but when I found the lifestyle, I knew it was for me. It gave me the control I needed. But it goes beyond that too. Dominants need to feel needed. Submissives need to feel wanted. The submissives at the club have needs I can take care of—without sex. I've had many D/s relationships over the years that didn't involve sex, dating, or anything other than making sure they got what they needed. For some, it involved the whip. With others, it was simply ordering them to do certain tasks."

Wrapping her hands around his wrists, she pinned them to the bed. They both knew she couldn't physically prevent him from escaping. But she had other ways of restraining him. One look at her beautiful eyes told him the commanding Domme was back, her painful trip down memory lane was over, and playtime had begun again. "Grab hold of the headboard, subbie. Be a good boy—don't let go, and you'll be rewarded."

Hell, yeah!

A CELL PHONE ringing pulled Charlotte from the deep sleep she'd been in. Beside her, Mike reached over to the nightstand on his side of the bed and silenced the loud noise before glancing at the screen. A blue glow reflected off his face as he read the caller ID. "Shit! My mother's neighbor."

He punched the answer button as Charlotte came fully

awake and sat up. She remained silent as he answered the call, concern filling his eyes. "Hello? Linda? What's wrong?" There was a pause, then a look of fear crossed his face. "A fire? Where—"

The woman must have cut him off. He listened as he flung the covers off his naked body and stood, snatching his neatly folded clothes from where he'd placed them atop of the hope chest. On the other side of the bed, Charlotte did the same and quickly got dressed.

"You're sure she's okay . . . all right, I'm on my way . . . and, Linda? Thank you." Disconnecting the call, he dropped the phone on the bed, grabbed his pants, and pulled them on. "She's with Linda. There's a fire in her kitchen, and the fire department is on the way. That's all I know. I have to go. Linda's calling Jake next."

In his frantic state, he clearly didn't realize she was coming with him. "I'll drive. You're in no shape to."

She'd half expected him to argue with her, but he nodded as he sat down on the bed and pulled on his sneakers. "Thanks."

Less than ten minutes later, Charlotte steered her SUV onto the street Mike had grown up on, although she couldn't park anywhere near his mom's house with all the police and fire department vehicles. Red and blue rotating lights bounced off every surface, and the neighbors were out of their homes, watching all the activity.

Charlotte pulled up behind a police car and had barely put it in Park before Mike jumped out the passenger side door and began running down the street. Climbing out, she waved him on when he glanced back over his shoulder. She knew he needed to see for himself that his mother was okay.

As she started to follow at a slower jog, the screech of tires had her spinning around. Jake sped down the street, slammed on the brakes, and parked his pickup behind her vehicle. Jake and Nick's panicked expressions, as they leaped from the truck, were the same as the one Mike had had on his face since getting the phone call.

The two men caught up with Charlotte, and together, they located Mike standing at the back of an ambulance, looking through the open rear doors. Collectively, they sighed in relief when they saw Emma Donovan sitting on a stretcher, arguing with the EMTs and Mike that she was perfectly fine and wasn't going to the hospital. She was in a floral nightgown, and a blanket was covering the lower half of her body. Her friend Linda was chatting with a few neighbors nearby while the police and firemen did their jobs.

From the sound of things, the fire was out, but there was smoke and water damage. The scene buzzed around them. The loud engines of the fire trucks and ambulance, shouted orders among the first responders, radios squawking, and all the other noise filling the air made quiet conversation nearly impossible.

"Mom, are you okay?" Jake asked, even though he'd heard her refusing the oxygen mask they were trying to put back over her face after she'd taken it off. "What the heck happened?"

"She was cooking and went to bed with the oven on and food in it!" Mike's angry, exasperated tone caused an embarrassed blush to cross his mother's cheeks. "Apparently, she didn't have her hearing aids in and didn't hear the damn smoke alarms. If it wasn't for that fireman, who moved in up the street last month, coming home after a late shift and seeing the smoke, God knows what would have happened. He kicked in the front door, got her out, called 9-1-1, and brought the garden hose into the kitchen to keep the fire from spreading."

"It was an accident, Michael," Emma rebuked. "And please

stop yelling—I'm not a child. It could have happened to anyone."

"That's—"

Mike stopped short when Charlotte placed a calming hand on his arm. He glanced at her, and she squeezed his arm before saying in a low voice, "Easy, Michael—she's okay. I know you're upset, but so is she. And she's scared too—don't add to her stress."

He hesitated, then nodded, running a hand down his face. "I'm sorry, Mom. You just scared the hell out of us."

When one of the crew members moved an equipment bag from the ambulance's rear bench, Jake climbed in, sat, and took hold of his mother's pale, shaking hand. He addressed the female EMT. "Does she have to go to the hospital?"

"Her vitals are good." She held up a stethoscope. "If her lungs are clear, then I don't see a reason for her to go."

Moments later, Nick and Mike helped Emma step down from the back of the rig just as the fire chief came looking for them. "You got lucky, ma'am. We were able to keep it confined to the kitchen. However, there's a lot of smoke and water damage, and we had to rip down most of your cabinets and drag the stove out to make sure the fire didn't spread through the walls. It turns out the builder put extra fire-proofing behind that whole wall, so it saved the rest of the house from going up. Unfortunately, the kitchen itself is pretty much a total loss. We'll make sure there won't be any potential flare-ups. The fire inspector and insurance adjusters can come out and look at it tomorrow, but you won't be able to stay there for a while. I'll give you a list of cleanup companies too."

Mike shook hands with the man. "Thanks. She'll be staying with me tonight."

As the chief left to check on his squad, Jake turned to his brother. "Why don't Nick and I take Mom back with us? She can stay in the spare bedroom, and the Trident women can fuss over her for the next few days. There'll be plenty of us to take care of her, and Nick and I can do some work from the apartment."

A heavy sigh escaped Mike. "All right. Then I'll take care of the inspector, insurance, and cleanup company."

"Good." Jake glanced over his shoulder at the house before turning back. "Nick, can you see if they'll let us in to get some clothes, her hearing aids, medications, and stuff. We can throw her clothes in the washing machine if they smell of smoke."

"Okay. It'll probably take a bit, though, until they're done in there. Why don't you take Emma back in your truck? I'll call Parker and see if he can send someone out to board up the doors and the kitchen window. Once that's done, I'll drive her car back to the compound."

Parker Christensen was a member of The Covenant, who owned a construction company and had plenty of men working for him and the supplies to get it done quickly, even in the middle of the night. In fact, he'd done all the renovations of the Trident compound buildings, including the club.

"But I still don't know where I put those damn car keys," Emma stated. "I've looked everywhere."

Sheepishly, Mike pulled two conjoined key rings from his pocket and separated them. "That's because I've had them. I was worried about you driving and knew you wouldn't give them up willingly."

"And here I was thinking I was getting Alzheimer's. Michael, how could you?"

He pulled her into his arms, ignoring her angry glare. "I did it because I love you, Mom. If something happened to you, and I could have prevented it, I'd never forgive myself."

Emma's shoulders relaxed as she embraced her son. She then pulled back and motioned for Nick and Jake to join them in a group hug. "You too, Charlotte. You're more than welcome to be a part of my crazy extended family. Thank you so much for being here for me and for Michael."

A warm, tingling feeling coursed through Charlotte, and it wasn't from the woman's words but from the gratitude she saw in Mike's eyes. She could tell it meant a lot for her to be here with him, even if he hadn't verbally told her so.

Charlotte joined the group, standing between Mike and Nick, before smiling at Emma. "I'm just glad you're okay, Mrs. Donovan. We were all so worried when we heard what happened."

"Please, call me Emma, Charlotte. And I don't ever want to worry any of you ever again. Jake, tomorrow we'll call that nice lady at Twin Ponds. I'll have to have the damage to the house fixed before I can sell it."

Jake's arm around the older woman's shoulders gave her a squeeze. "We'll get Parker's company on it right away, then get it listed. In this neighborhood, I'm sure it'll sell quickly. Don't you worry about a thing."

Emma pursed her lips, and tears filled her eyes as she looked back and forth between her two sons. "I probably should have gotten rid of it years ago. There are some very bad memories in that house for both of you. I'm so sorry I didn't have the courage to stand up to your father back then. He was a good husband but not a good father. I'm sorry."

Leaning down, Mike kissed his mother's forehead. "It's not your fault, Mom. I doubt either of us can ever forgive and forget what he did, but you always made sure we knew you loved us. And right now, that's all that's important—that we love each other and are there for each other."

"Amen," Jake added.

Leaving Nick to get whatever of Emma's he could to hold her over for a few days, the other three walked Emma to Jake's truck. After making sure she was settled into the passenger seat, Mike gave her another kiss on the cheek and shut the door. Once he and Charlotte climbed into her SUV, Mike grabbed her hand before she could put the key in the ignition. She raised her brow at him. "Something wrong?"

"No. Well, except for the obvious, of course. I just wanted to say thank you." Charlotte relaxed under his gentle gaze as he continued. "I didn't quite understand it when Nick said that Jake grounded him when he was stressed, but now I get it. When you touched me and told me to go easy on my mom, it grounded me. You gave me something to hold onto when I felt like I was spiraling out of control. I could breathe and think again instead of worrying about everything that could've happened instead of what did. I was so freaked out about the fire and the damage and the fact she could have been killed, but you soothed me and made me realize the only thing that mattered was she was alive and unhurt. Everything else takes a backseat to that. So, again, thank you for being here for me."

Reaching up, she cupped his cheek. Her heart swelled as she smiled at him. "There's no place else I'd rather be, Michael. Let's go home."

Fourteen

Grabbing the glass of wine she'd been nursing for the past hour, Charlotte strode down the bar and sat on the stool next to Jenn Mullins as two of the other waitresses got up to go to the ladies' room. The party Mike and the pub staff had thrown to celebrate her moving on to bigger and better things was winding down. They'd done it on a Monday night because it was the slowest day of the week, and The Covenant was closed, so some of the people who worked there, who Jenn had gotten to know through her surrogate uncles, could also attend.

As far as Charlotte knew, the young woman had never been inside the club, at least while it was open. Her godfather, Ian, would probably have a heart attack if Jenn got interested in the lifestyle. While there was nothing wrong with it, in general, her uncles had been such a huge part of her life, and there was no way they wanted to see her or be seen by her in the sex club.

It had been six days since the fire at Emma Donovan's house. Things had been crazy since then. Two of Charlotte's parolees had gotten arrested in separate incidents. Another had gone AWOL with a teenage girl two days ago. They were on a cross-state crime spree, robbing several stores and carjacking at least three vehicles. So far, the victims had only reported a few minor injuries, but Charlotte and the cops chasing the modern-day Bonnie and Clyde knew they were escalating. When the law caught up with them, Charlotte had a strong feeling it would end badly.

Mike was also dealing with a lot lately. After the fire the other night at Emma's, he'd spent the next few days handling all the details that went into getting the house restored and prepared to sell. He'd had meetings with the fire inspector, insurance adjuster, Parker and his architect, and the assisted living staff to plan for Emma's move into the facility next Friday.

Add in everything he had to do to run the pub, he'd hardly had any free time during the day. But each night, Charlotte had invited him into her bed, where he'd stayed until sunrise. He'd needed her—even if it was simply to cuddle next to her while he slept—and she'd been more than willing to be there for him. However, when things calmed down again, she wasn't sure she wanted to let him return to his condo to sleep at night. She was falling for him—and for the first time since she'd entered the lifestyle, she was nervous about being honest with a sub.

As Charlotte got comfortable on the seat next to Jenn, she glanced down to the other end of the bar, where the younger, blonde woman's gaze was focused on a handsome man who was chatting with Jake and Nick. Doug Henderson was an employee of Trident Security and ran their Personal Protective Division.

When he'd worked for his former boss, Chase Dixon, at Blackhawk Security, he'd been contracted not once but twice to serve as Jenn's bodyguard when things had gone to shit. Once was when a hitman had been hired to take out several former members of SEAL Team Four—unfortunately, Jenn's mother and retired-SEAL father had been murdered before Ian, Devon, and the others had figured out what was going on. The second time had been when Ian's then-girlfriend, now wife, had become a target when dirty DEA agents had hunted her best friend.

"Does he know you're interested in him?" Charlotte asked.

Jenn startled, ripping her gaze from the object of her obvious affection—obvious, at least, to another woman. The men in the room, including Henderson, were probably oblivious. "Huh? Wh0?"

"Don't play dumb, Jenn. You're far too smart for that."

Sighing, Jenn slumped her shoulders. "No, he doesn't. He treats me like a kid in high school. I'm twenty-two, almost done with college, and have dealt with more crap than most people will deal with in a lifetime. I'm old enough to date anyone I want."

Charlotte smiled. "And Doug is, what, thirty?"

"Yeah. It doesn't help that he works for Uncle Ian and Uncle Dev, either. They'd never let any of their employees date me—if any of them were even interested." She snorted. "In fact, I'd be surprised it's not in some employment contract they have to sign."

Yeah, that was probably not too far from the truth. The Sexy Six-Pack—as Devon's wife Kristen had dubbed him, Ian, Brody, Jake, Marco, and Boomer—tended to be very overprotective of their loved ones.

Charlotte patted Jenn's hand. "Don't worry. If it's meant to be, it'll happen. For now, concentrate on finishing up your degree, getting through your internship, and just enjoying life. Someday down the road, one of two things will happen. One, Doug will get hit by Cupid's arrow and realize you're no longer the teenager he'd first met a few years ago. Or, two, you'll meet someone else and realize *he's* your soulmate, not Doug."

Jenn gave her a sideways glance before taking a sip of her Malibu Bay Breeze. "Do you really believe in soulmates?"

"Sure. Look at all your uncles. They've all met theirs—the one person they couldn't imagine life without. The one person who they'd sacrifice everything for."

The younger woman mulled that over for a moment before asking, "So, what about you, Charlotte? You and Mike seem to be seeing a lot of each other lately. Do you think he might be your soulmate?"

Was he? Charlotte had no idea. If they went their separate ways tomorrow, would she have a hole in her heart? Would she feel like the best thing that had and could ever happen to her was gone? Did she want to find out the hard way?

Standing, she smirked at the younger woman with a confidence she didn't feel. "When I figure that out, you'll be the third person to know."

Jenn laughed as Charlotte walked away.

JUST AFTER 11:00 P.M., Mike waved goodbye to Ian, Devon, and their wives as they headed out the front door of the pub. Most of the party-goers had left, but there were still a few stragglers who showed no sign of wanting to leave. That was okay with him, though. Mike had needed a fun night to relax after the stressful week he'd had.

Still spread out along the bar were Jake, Nick, Jenn, Charlotte, Reggie Helm, a Dom at the club, his wife, Colleen, Trident Security's office manager, Doug Henderson, and the new waitress, Daniella. The rest of the staff, Jenn's extended family, a few friends, and several regular customers had all started dwindling over the past hour. Monday nights tended to have a skeleton crew, but a few of the employees who'd been off or worked during the day had also stopped in to say goodbye to Jenn.

About a half-hour earlier, Mike had told the bartender to go home. She hadn't been feeling well, and most of the cleanup had already been handled. She'd been grateful and thanked him profusely before heading out the back door of the pub. The staff parked their vehicles behind the building to leave the spaces out front for the customers.

Mike lowered the volume of the jukebox, which suddenly seemed loud with fewer people in the large room, then checked everyone's drinks. Jenn and Daniella were sitting and chatting at the far end of the long, wooden bar while the others were gathered toward the middle of it. He noticed Charlotte's glass of tonic water and lime she'd switched over to was only a third full, so he picked up the glass and refilled it.

"Hey, Mike," Nick said. "I know the oven and stuff are shut down, but what are the chances of getting some chips and salsa?"

Jake snorted and put his arm across his fiancé's shoulders. "I honestly have no idea where he puts all the damn food he eats."

Patting his rock-hard abs, Nick smirked. "I'm a bottomless pit and proud of it."

"Yeah, tell me that again in about twenty years when your metabolism changes."

Mike chuckled at the two of them as he strode to the kitchen, which had been left spotless by the staff, as usual. In the huge, commercial-sized refrigerator, he found the jar of homemade salsa the new sous chef had made the day before and set it on the counter. He was just about to retrieve a bag of tortilla chips from the pantry when the back door to the alley swung open. Confusion quickly morphed into terror when four masked men rushed in, pointing black, ugly handguns at him.

Oh shit!

Before Mike could sound the alarm to the others in the bar, the first guy through the door thrust a gun in his face. It might sound cliché, but Mike's life passed before his eyes. And the best part of it had been after a beautiful Domme had set her sights on him.

"Don't say a fucking word," the man warned, his voice muffled by the mask. "And keep your hands where I can see them." He pushed Mike toward the swinging door to the bar. "Move!"

As the four men followed him, Mike kept his empty hands at shoulder height and tried to figure out what the fuck was going on. He hated the feeling of helplessness that came over him as he walked through the door. Charlotte, Jake, and the others had the same flash of confusion in their eyes before the weapons pointed in their direction registered in their brains. After that, it was a mix of reactions. Jenn and Daniella had looks of horror on their faces as they held onto each other. Reggie stepped in front of his gaping wife, the lawyer ready to slay dragons for her if he had to. Jake, Nick, Henderson, and Charlotte, however, had frozen—not in fear, but in a manner that told Mike each was assessing the situation and analyzing how to end it without no one but the bad guys bleeding or worse.

Charlotte may not have had the military training the three men standing beside her had undergone, but one wouldn't know that by looking at her. Her eyes had that same "you're fucking with the wrong people" glare in them. Mike knew she was carrying her weapon hidden on her body, and so were Nick, Jake, and Henderson, but no one moved to draw them. They'd wait until they were certain they'd gained a tactical advantage instead of having a shootout with unarmed people in their midst.

A hand shoved Mike forward, and a growl came from one of the men behind him. "What the fuck? You said he'd be fucking alone, or there'd only be a bartender this time of night."

"That's all there usually is!" a second man responded, the nervousness in his voice a huge contrast to the pissed-off tone of his buddy. It was also awfully familiar, despite the mask muffling it.

Mike saw a flare of recognition in Charlotte's eyes before it disappeared again. *Damn it.* His success in hiring an ex-con just dropped from batting .500 to .333—not bad for the Major Leagues, but it sucked at Donovan's.

"Look, you can take the money or whatever you want," Mike said with a calmness he didn't feel. "There's no need to shoot anyone."

"Shut the fuck up!" The tallest of the four was apparently the ringleader and, as such, was the one they didn't want to piss off. "Get on the fucking floor, now! All of you!"

Jake held up his hands in a placating manner. "All right. Just chill. Everyone, do as he says."

They all lowered themselves to the ground slowly—Mike near the kitchen door with his two waitresses and the others in the middle of the room by the bar. Once they were all down, the ringleader strode toward the front door and locked it. "Bring the shit in, and let's get this done."

The nervous guy and one of the others returned to the kitchen, and Mike's brow wasn't the only one furrowing in confusion.

"Bring the shit in"? What the hell is going on? Is it a robbery or not?

Returning to the far end of the bar, the leader bent down and grabbed Daniella by the hair. She screeched in pain as he forced her to stand. Growls came from the Dominants in the room, in addition to Doug, and Mike started to get up from the floor to help his employee. "Leave her—"

"Shut the fuck up and get down on the floor!" He held the gun to Daniella's head, and whatever color had still been in her cheeks drained. Her eyes wide in fear, she tried to keep herself close to the man to ease the pain in her scalp. After Mike laid down on his stomach again, the punk gestured to the others on the floor and barked at his friend. "Search them and grab their cell phones. I don't want any fucking surprises or anyone calling the cops. If any of you move, I'll put a bullet in this bitch."

Mike didn't know how his brother, Nick, Doug, and Charlotte stayed so calm, but it had to be from their training. Meanwhile, the rest of the hostages seemed to be barely holding things together. When asshole number two patted down Jake, he found a 9mm at the operative's lower back. Pulling it out of the holster, he pointed it at Jake's head. "What the fuck? Are you a fucking cop?"

"No! He's not!" With his mask still on, Jose had returned with the fourth accomplice and a bunch of equipment that confused Mike even more. "He's a—a bodyguard—not a cop! He's the owner's brother."

"Bodyguard, huh?" He nudged Jake's thigh with his foot. "Think you're a tough guy? Try anything stupid, and I'll pump you full of lead."

Jake glared at him. "I'm not looking to get shot, but you should know those two guys and the lady in the red shirt work with me, and they're probably carrying too." He'd jutted his chin toward Doug, Nick, and Charlotte.

Stunned, it took Mike a moment to realize his brother knew the guy was going to find the weapons on the other three anyway, and as much as Jake had probably hated to announce they were armed, it was for the best. That way, these punks wouldn't think any of them were cops and shoot them on principle.

Mike was glad Charlotte's state ID and shield were in her purse behind the bar where he'd put it for safekeeping. What he couldn't figure out was why Jose had stepped in and possibly saved Jake from being killed. The ex-con had met Jake and Nick the other night when they'd stopped in for dinner—maybe that was why.

Charlotte had told Mike about her suspicions that his new employee might be in trouble—looks like she'd been absolutely right. Even if the two of them hadn't already figured out who Jose was, it was now obvious to everyone in the room that he knew them—and in return, they knew him.

Hopefully, his cohorts didn't figure that out, too. They were covering their faces, and Mike had seen enough movies and TV shows to pray it meant they didn't plan on killing anyone as long as they couldn't be identified later. If only Mike could get behind the bar where there were two silent alarm buttons. One was near where the waitresses placed their orders at the rear end of the bar, and the other was below the register closest to the front of the room.

Once everyone had been searched and stripped of any weapons and cell phones, the leader released Daniella. He glanced around and stepped over to the entrance to the darkened party room. Finding the light switch, he flipped it up, bathing the room in a soft glow from the overhead recessed lights. The prick pointed at Daniella and Jenn. "Get in there."

Scared, Jenn looked at her Uncle Jake, her wide eyes brimming with tears that hadn't spilled over yet. With a stoic expression, he nodded. "Go ahead, Baby-girl. It'll be alright."

She stood and held Daniella's shaking hand as they cautiously disappeared from Mike's view into the smaller room.

The leader snarled. "Sit down." He then waved his gun toward the others. "You two bitches get in there too."

Slowly, Charlotte got to her feet, and Mike could tell she wanted to kick some serious ass but had to wait for an opportunity. And it scared the hell out of him. If something happened to her, he didn't know what he'd do. He couldn't deny it anymore. Sometime between her birthday party and tonight, he'd fallen in love with her. And now, they were all in danger and still had no idea what was happening.

Charlotte put her arm around Colleen's shoulders and walked with her across the expanse toward the party room. As they passed Mike, Charlotte glanced down at him. It was then he saw the fear hidden behind her brave front, and he tried to give her a reassuring smile. Somehow, he knew she was more afraid for him and the others than for herself. She had that same nature Mike saw in his brother.

Jake had always said if he died trying to save an innocent's life, it would be worth it. Now, it was clear to Mike that Charlotte would martyr herself if the choice came down to her or someone she cared about. God help him if that happened. He couldn't let her do that for him and would do everything he could to ensure she never had to make that choice for anyone else.

Fifteen

Charlotte let go of Colleen, and they took seats at the table the masked ringleader had pointed at. Jenn and Daniella sat across from them. Shifting her chair, Charlotte angled it so she could still see most of what was happening in the other room. The leader and the guy who'd searched everyone had aimed their weapons at Jake, Nick, Doug, Reggie, and Mike as they were each ordered to stand and sit at one of the round tables not far from the party room. Although they'd probably done that to keep an eye on both the men and women simultaneously, it also gave Charlotte a way to communicate with Jake and Nick without being obvious.

Thank God she'd participated in some of their team sessions at the Trident compound. She'd gotten a kick out of searching for bad guys with them in their training building and the Hogan's Alley they'd set up. She'd learned hand signals from the retired SEALs, and while she didn't know a lot, hopefully, she knew enough to devise some sort of plan. But first, they had to figure out what Jose and his buddies were up to. The one thing she'd zeroed in on already was that her parolee was unhappy about being involved in whatever it was. He was nervous, possibly to the point of being scared shitless, and didn't seem to want to be there at all. So, the question was, why *was* he involved?

Jose and the fourth masked suspect came into the party room carrying a folding ladder from the pub's storage room and a large duffel bag. Charlotte's parolee glanced nervously at her before looking away again. He had to know that no matter what happened, at this point, he was fucked.

The two men passed the women and then pushed an unoccupied table and chairs away from the wall opposite the doorway. As they began to set up the ladder, Charlotte realized what they were up to.

Well, shit.

The robbery was turning into a burglary—a drug heist, to be specific. She watched Jose steady the ladder while the other man climbed up and popped out several ceiling tiles. Reaching up into the darkness, he grabbed a construction beam and hauled himself into the empty space. Jose pulled a crowbar from the duffel bag and handed it up to the other man.

They were breaking into the pharmacy next door. From what Charlotte could figure, on the other side of that section of the wall was where the prescription drugs were stored. The front and rear doors of the pharmacy were probably wired with an alarm. However, since the shop had been there for over thirty or forty years, it most likely didn't have an interior alarm system with motion sensors or any extra features other than a silent alarm button. Going through the ceiling would allow the suspects to drop down and have plenty of time to get what they were looking for before someone noticed there was a break-in.

The martial arts studio on the other side of the pharmacy had huge plate-glass windows and kept low lights on inside when the place was closed. Charlotte didn't know if it had an alarm system, but regardless, a person inside could be seen by anyone passing by. So, it seemed these guys had figured out a way to get around all the alarms, but they hadn't counted on a few party-goers still being inside the pub with the owner. On a Monday night, Mike usually closed down around 10-10:30 since it wasn't a busy time of the week. Jose had been off from kitchen duty tonight, so either he hadn't heard about the going-away party or had forgotten—not that it mattered now.

What did matter now was how to end this with the bad guys in jail and not a scratch on the good guys and innocents. Jake had done the right thing by outing the fact that Nick, Doug, and Charlotte had been carrying weapons. If Jose's buddies thought any of them were cops, they might have panicked and gotten rid of the witnesses. Charlotte just prayed that wasn't their plan to begin with.

She glanced at Mike and saw he was staring at her intently. She gave him a small, reassuring smile, which he returned, causing her heart to skip a beat. If they got out of this alive, she would tell him how she really felt about him. What they had between them was something she never thought she'd find. A good man who was her equal yet still understood what she needed in the bedroom. She'd fallen in love with Mike, the big lug, and it was time he heard that from her. She just hoped he felt the same.

Next to Charlotte, Colleen scooted her chair closer to her. The younger woman waited until none of the suspects were paying attention to her before leaning over and whispering. "My gun is in my purse on the back of the barstool I was sitting on. If we can get Reggie to have an asthma attack, I can say I have to get his inhaler from it, then bring the purse in here to you. You're a much better shot."

The sweet submissive had come a long way since she'd

first started working for Trident Security. The men there had taken her under their wings, with Reggie's consent, and taught her how to defend herself, stay calm in tense situations, and even shoot. Ian had insisted she get her carry license since they never knew when a case would come back and bite them on the ass, and he wanted her protected.

With a dip of her chin, Charlotte acknowledged the other woman. She wasn't sure it would work but didn't have any other ideas of how to go up against four men with guns—well, three at the moment. The fourth was somewhere above or in the pharmacy.

Charlotte assessed where the suspects stood and what they were doing. One was checking the parking lot through the front window curtains. Jose stood next to the ladder, looking up into the crawlspace, probably waiting to hear what the other guy needed. The ringleader was pacing back and forth, his gaze darting everywhere. If Charlotte had to guess, she'd say the guy was juiced up on something, and that was both a good and bad thing. Good, because he couldn't focus on one thing for long. Bad, because he could be trigger-happy.

Coughing, she caught Jake's attention. Unfortunately, she had to wait a moment because the ringleader glared at her as if her cough had annoyed the hell out of him. Once he began pacing again, Charlotte nodded once at Jake, then tilted her head to her right, his left, to indicate Reggie, who was sitting next to him. When Jake signaled for her to continue, she put her hand to her chest and took several deep breaths. Glancing at the ringleader to make sure he wasn't watching —he was grabbing a bottle of whiskey from behind the bar— Charlotte mimed using an inhaler, then made a gun with her fingers, hoping Jake would figure out the rest.

Without taking his gaze off of her, he mouthed the word "asthma," and Charlotte realized he'd actually whispered it only loud enough for Reggie to hear him. The lawyer narrowed his eyes at Jake, who then clarified. "Fake an asthma attack."

Reggie's gaze shot to Charlotte and then his wife, who gestured using an inhaler. He finally got it and nodded. Pushing his chair back loudly, he took several deep breaths and brought his hand to his chest. The ringleader came from around the bar, his weapon in one hand, a bottle of Jack Daniels in the other, and glared at him. "What the fuck are you doing?"

Gasping and pulling at the collar of his shirt, Reggie could've been an actor as he rasped, "I-I can't breathe."

The men sitting at the table gave appropriate looks of concern, and Jake asked, "Where's your inhaler, Reggie?"

"C-Colleen's . . . got it . . . need it."

His wife stood, and the ringleader turned his gun toward her. "Where do you think you're going, bitch?"

She took a brave step forward. "Please, he needs his inhaler. I have it in my purse." Colleen pointed to where her bag hung from the back of a bar stool and took a few more steps until she stood in the doorway between the two rooms. "Please, let me get it. H-he just needs to take a few puffs, and he'll be fine."

The perp glanced from her to the stool to Reggie, who was doing a fine job of pretending he couldn't breathe—at least, Charlotte hoped it was still an act. The lawyer looked awfully pale. Finally, the gang leader looked at Colleen again. "Fine. Anything to shut him up. But don't try anything stupid."

"I-I won't." Without hesitation, Colleen hurried over to the bar and snatched her purse from the back of the stool. Shuffling through it, she found the inhaler and pulled it out. Hanging her purse from her shoulder and tucking it close to her side, in a move natural for most women, Colleen proceeded to the table where the men were sitting. She handed the inhaler to her husband under the watchful eye of the two perps in that room. "Here, Reggie. Take a few puffs."

A loud noise from the other side of the wall behind Charlotte had everyone turning in that direction. Grabbing Colleen's upper arm, the ringleader dragged her back to the party room and shoved her toward the chair she'd been sitting in. He yelled over his shoulder to the punk at the front of the bar. "Watch them!"

He continued over to the ladder, pushed Jose out of the way, and climbed up to the top. "What the fuck are you doing over there?"

His accomplice cursed. "What do you fucking think I'm trying to do? I'm trying to get the damn . . . arrgghhh . . . cabinet open."

"Well, hurry the fuck up!"

Charlotte used the distraction to take the Sig Sauer P320 Subcompact Colleen had furtively removed from its holster in her purse. The small, 9mm held twelve bullets and fit neatly in the parole officer's hand. She expertly flipped the safety off, then tucked the weapon into the waistband of her jeans, under her shirt. Against her bare skin, the cold, sharp metal was uncomfortable and risky with the safety off, but she could draw it easily and fire if needed.

The grinding of metal against metal was followed by another loud bang over in the pharmacy. "Got it!"

The ringleader snorted. "'Bout fucking time! Get the shit, and let's get out of here!"

Stepping down from the ladder, he sauntered back to the table the women were sitting at as if he didn't have a care in the world now that they'd gained access to the drugs. His demeanor had changed again—he was definitely on something. He smirked at Jenn. Using the hand that was still holding the bottle of Jack, he ran a finger down her cheek, ignoring her flinch and hard eyes. "Whatta ya say, sweet thing? Want to come party with us?"

"Not on your fucking life, jackass," the pretty blonde growled. Channeling her Uncle Ian, she smacked his hand away.

The prick slammed the bottle onto the table and grabbed Jenn by the hair, yanking her head back. "Bitch!"

In the next few moments, so much happened at once. Jenn screeched in pain. In the other room, Doug leaped from his seat, sending the chair flying backward, his face red with rage. "Get your fucking hands off her!"

The suspect who'd been watching the men swung his weapon around to shoot Doug, but Nick was faster, snatching an unlit candle in a heavy, round holder from the table and throwing it at the guy's head. Simultaneously, Jake kicked out from where he sat and smashed the bastard's knee with the heel of his boot-covered foot. When the gun went off, the bullet slammed into the ceiling, and the shooter screamed in agony and dropped to the floor. The two former SEALs had him disarmed and restrained within seconds.

Meanwhile, at the same time, Charlotte also stood quickly, reaching for the gun at her lower back, but the ringleader hauled Jenn out of her chair and sent her crashing into the table. The table knocked into Charlotte, and the chair she'd stood from tipped over and got tangled in her legs, making her lose her balance and stumble. Twisting, she fell on her ass, causing pain to explode in her tailbone. Fury flared in the ringleader's eyes through the cutouts in the mask as he shoved Jenn aside and raised his gun.

"No!" Jose yelled, lunging forward and pulling out the gun he'd stuck in his front waistband.

Instead of shooting Charlotte, the leader spun on the new threat and pulled the trigger. The bullet slammed into Jose's chest. Stunned, he froze before falling to his knees. Screams and shouts filled the air. Before the drugged-up bastard could bring his gun back around completely, Charlotte fired. His head snapped back as the slug hit him between the eyes. He was dead before he hit the ground.

The next thing Charlotte knew, Mike was lifting her to her feet. "Are you okay? Shit, Charlotte, tell me you're okay." His shaking hands and panicked gaze roamed her body, looking for any sign she was injured.

"I-I'm fine. Jenn? Daniella? Colleen?" She looked at each one of them, making sure none had been shot. Doug already had his arms around Jenn, holding the trembling young woman as she buried her face in his chest. Embracing, Colleen and Reggie assured each other they were okay. Jake checked on Daniella, while in the other room, Nick held the other suspect at gunpoint.

The guy in the pharmacy yelled, "What the hell's going on? Ace? Jose?" But no one answered him.

Charlotte's ears were ringing from the loud gun reports. Scanning the room, she finally realized Jose was lying on the ground, covered in blood. "Damn it."

She pulled from Mike's arms, set the gun on the table, and rushed over to where the young man was gasping for air. Mike was right behind her, telling Jake to call 9-1-1 and grabbing a clean tablecloth from one of the empty tables. Charlotte took it from him and put pressure on the wound, but it was clear Jose was fading fast.

He stared up at her with pain- and tear-filled eyes. "I-I'm so-sorry, Ms. Roth. Th-they have Dina and . . . and Tomas. Ma-made me do it . . . said they'd k-kill them."

Shit. "Where are they, Jose?"

"D-don't know . . . Ace has som-someone watching . . . them." He swallowed hard, his breath becoming more labored. "Pl-Please save th-them . . . tell them I-I'm s-sorry."

Behind her, Charlotte heard Jake giving out orders. He

took over the watch of the one suspect and sent Nick and Doug out to the alleyway to see if they could grab the other. The guy was still shouting from the pharmacy, trying to figure out what had gone wrong. They'd have to wait until he came out of the rear exit, which was locked from the inside, but it wouldn't take long. A getaway vehicle was probably parked back there. Once he realized his buddies weren't going to be able to help him, he'd want to get the hell out of there. There was no honor among thieves.

"We'll find them, Jose, I promise. Just stay with me. Help is on the way."

"Not—not gonna make . . . it. Tell them . . . I love them, and I'm so—" Jose stilled as his last breath left him. His lifeless eyes open, seeing nothing.

Unexpected tears rolled down Charlotte's cheek. She wished she could have done something to save him, but from the amount of blood pouring out of the entrance and exit wounds on his chest and back, it'd been hopeless from the start. The bullet had probably hit a major artery—he'd bled out in under two minutes.

Charlotte rested back on her heels. Hands cupped her shoulders from behind, and she glanced back. She hadn't realized Mike had stood. He tightened his grip and pulled her up. Ignoring the blood now covering both their hands, he wrapped his arms around her. A sob escaped her, followed by another as Charlotte buried her face into his chest.

Mike kissed the top of her head. "It's my turn to take care of you, baby. I've got you . . . I've got you."

Sixteen

"How are you doing, Michael?" Charlotte purred as she led her sub around the pit. It was his first night in the club with play privileges and his third visit to The Covenant during open hours. However, he was still like a kid in a candy store. His wide-eyed gaze was all over the place as he gaped at one scene after another, still trying to wrap his brain around the different types of play. She chuckled to herself. Pretty much everyone new to the lifestyle reacted the same way during their first few visits to a club.

"I'm good, Mistress Charlotte." He frowned as he looked down at her. "Am I doing anything wrong?"

"Not at all." Giving him a saucy smile, she ran her fingers down his bare chest. He'd dressed in a faded pair of snug jeans and nothing else, as per her orders. She knew it would take him a while to get used to being in public with fewer clothes on. However, for now, that was fine with her. She liked knowing she was the only one who got to see him completely naked. "But don't worry—I'll look forward to punishing you if you do."

"Thank you, Ma'am. I'm sure I'll look forward to it too."

The corners of his mouth ticked upward, but the smile didn't quite reach his eyes, and her gut clenched. Something had been bothering him for the last few days—he'd been quieter than normal— and although she'd asked him several times if something was wrong, he'd only stated he had a lot on his mind. She'd debated whether or not to push him further but had held off until now—wanting to see if he'd spill his guts without her persuasion. It was her responsibility to ensure the emotional well-being of her sub was taken care of. His evasive behavior would cease tonight. Once they got into the playroom, all bets were off. They weren't going to leave there until she knew what was wrong —only then would she know how to resolve it.

She strode past several more scenes, and he respectfully stayed on her heels. She'd gone through the club protocols extensively before his first trip to the club. She knew some things would take him out of his comfort zone and would be awkward for him at first, but she'd also agreed to no public humiliation in their contract. Many of the subs she'd been in contracts with before had wanted that, so she'd complied—it hadn't mattered to her one way or the other. It'd been all about giving them what they needed. But with Michael, his needs were different than the masochists in the club, and she'd gladly modified for him. That didn't mean she wasn't going to push his limits.

It had been just over two weeks since Jenn's party had ended in bloodshed. After the police had arrived and taken the two remaining suspects into custody, it hadn't taken Detective Isaac Webb and his partner long to find out where Jose's fiancée and child were being held. The local SWAT team had been dispatched, and the hostages were rescued without further violence.

After Jake had called 9-1-1 that night, his next calls had been to Ian and the rest of his teammates. They'd all shown up at the pub as fast as they could. Kat had been the lone significant other to come along. Boomer had allowed his wife to accompany him only after being assured the danger was all over. All the other Trident women, either pregnant or with little ones, had stayed home, impatiently waiting for word that everyone really was okay.

While the hostages had all seemingly recovered from their ordeal, Charlotte knew Jenn was feeling more frustrated than ever about Doug Henderson. The man had comforted Ian's goddaughter and held her tightly in those minutes following the gunshots, but after the rest of her uncles had arrived on the scene, the bodyguard had put distance between them again. Jenn's disappointment had been evident—at least to Charlotte—but she also hadn't seen what the Domme had noticed. There'd been a silent war raging in the man's eyes. He felt more for Jenn than the young woman realized, and for some unknown reason, he was fighting it. Was it the age difference between them or the fact she was his boss's goddaughter? If Charlotte had to guess, it was a little of both.

The pub had been closed for three days—two for the police investigation and one more for a crime scene cleanup company to expunge all evidence of the incident from public scrutiny. Brody Evans had retrieved the video and audio recordings from the pub's security system he'd designed and handed them over to the detectives. The footage had told the whole story and satisfied the district attorney that no one other than the two remaining suspects would be charged in the events leading to the deaths of their comrades.

Mike ensured all his employees were compensated for their unexpected time off. He was once again looking for a new sous chef and had surprised Charlotte by saying he would still consider another ex-con. His reasoning was if it hadn't been for the threat against his family, Jose probably would have been with him for a long time. He'd been a hard worker, looking to better his lot in life, and had gotten caught up in a situation where most people would have responded the same way—by doing what they thought best to save their loved ones.

As for the young widow, there was no family she was close to, and Jake had been worried she might be subjected to a vengeful retaliation from the rest of Ace's gang. Calling in a favor, Jake had arranged for her and her son to be relocated to another state through an organization called Friends of Patty. While they usually helped victims of domestic violence to disappear for their own safety, the local chapter had agreed it would be best to help Jose's fiancée and child start over somewhere else.

Stopping at an occupied spanking bench where Devon Sawyer had his wife strapped down, Charlotte snatched a pillow from a nearby chair and dropped it at her feet. "Kneel and watch, my sweet."

Pride and satisfaction welled within her as Mike didn't hesitate to do her bidding. She'd upped his training, and it appeared the difference between private and public play hadn't bothered him regarding certain commands. After his initial unease on the first night they'd walked around the crowded club, he'd relaxed. It'd helped when he'd realized no one there thought less of him for submitting to a Domme. In fact, there'd been appreciative looks sent his way from several women and men who were either Dominants or submissives. He'd stepped up his workouts with Jake, Nick, and some of the other Trident Security men on most mornings, and his abs were more noticeably cut. Charlotte loved them but had made sure he'd been doing it for himself and not just to impress her. Since he'd been working out for months before they entered their relationship, she'd believed him when he'd said it was 75% for himself and 25% for her.

Had the numbers been different, she may have thought he was lying.

The club was in full swing tonight. Between the people in the pit, bar area, and garden, there had to be over 200 members present, and that didn't include whoever was already playing in the two dozen private playrooms. Charlotte had reserved one of them for her and Mike. They had another fifteen minutes or so for the room to be free and cleaned—enough time to watch the scene before them.

As Master Devon spanked his pretty wife's bare ass with a paddle, Charlotte moved closer to Mike so her leg brushed against his arm. When he glanced up at her, she nodded once, and he wrapped his arm around her calf, gently stroking her skin. She'd found out he enjoyed touching her as much as possible. With some subs, she would have deduced they were "clingy," but not so with Mike. It just pleased him to have that physical connection between them, especially after their ordeal. Many nights they'd just cuddled on the couch at her house or his condo, binging on some Netflix shows and Häagen-Dazs. It turned out Mike was just as comfortable being a homebody as Charlotte was.

On nights when he'd worked late at the pub, they'd talk on the phone for a bit before she started to feel sleep pulling her under. She couldn't remember the last time she'd spent so much time talking and hanging out with her submissive outside of play, but Mike had become much more than just her submissive. He'd wormed his way into her heart. Her entertaining distraction had become a permanent one.

With her other subs, it had been easy to dismiss them in her mind while she'd been at work. However, thoughts of Mike were constantly popping into her brain throughout the day. She found her heart rate spiking any time her cell phone pinged with a text or the screen announced an incoming call from him. Sometimes it was to ask a question. Other times, it was just him wanting to say hello and hear her voice.

Placing her hand on Mike's head, Charlotte stroked his hair as Master Devon reddened Kristen's ass. Charlotte knew why the Dom was subjecting his sub to a public spanking tonight, even though it was on her yellow limit list, and he didn't do it often. He'd been frustrated to find out she was overstressed and not sleeping well and had been hiding those facts from him.

With caring for their infant son, a deadline for her latest book coming up, signing events, Devon's busy work schedule, and their lack of playtime lately, she hadn't wanted to tell him she was nearing a meltdown. When Devon had overheard her crying to Angie and Fancy, he'd been angry but more concerned than anything. As her Dom, *he* should have been the first person she'd told—it was his responsibility to take care of her, and he couldn't do that properly if she hid things from him. So, tonight, she was paying for it and being reminded that lying to her Dom by omission was still lying. The punishment would also give her the release she needed to destress.

Another *crack* sounded, followed by Kristen's shrieking, "Eleven!" A choked sob escaped her as tears rolled down her face. Devon stroked her back as he leaned down close to her head and spoke softly to her. After several nods of her head and words that no one but her Dom could hear over the club's music, he retook his position behind the bench and swatted her ass again. "Twelve!"

Charlotte glanced down and frowned. Mike's gaze was on the scene, but he didn't appear focused on it—his mind was elsewhere. She'd been walking around with a crop in her hand, mainly because it went with her sadistic, dominant persona, and she touched the tip of it to the underside of her sub's chin and lifted. His gaze rose to hers, and her heart clenched when she saw the anxiety in his eyes despite the smile he gave her.

Damn it.

Kristen wasn't the only one hiding things from her Dom. It was time for Charlotte to find out what was bothering Mike. Checking the small watch she had clipped to a belt loop on her black leather pencil skirt, she saw their room should be ready. She held out her hand, and Mike took it and got to his feet. Without a word, he followed her to the playrooms.

WITH EVERY STEP he took bringing him closer to the playrooms, Mike's anxiety grew. In three days, the contract he and Charlotte had signed would be up, and not once had she mentioned renewing it. If she didn't want to sign a new contract, Mike didn't know what he would do. He'd fallen head over heels for his pretty Domme but doubted she felt the same. Yeah, they'd spent a lot of time together the past few weeks, but any time the question about their future was on the tip of his tongue, he'd swallowed it. Never had he felt the loss of a woman deep in his soul. However, that's what he felt now, and he hadn't exactly lost Charlotte yet—but he would in three days. That is unless he manned up and told her how he felt while praying she didn't shoot him down.

Nick had told him the Domme rarely "dated" a sub, so maybe Mike had that in his favor. And they were definitely dating. Play was not the only thing on the agenda when they got together, and snuggling together on the couch, watching TV, and pigging out on ice cream had quickly become one of his favorite things to do with her.

After they entered their assigned playroom, Charlotte closed the door behind them, and the volume of the club music dropped dramatically. Mike glanced around and figured out this room's theme was a classroom—well, if classrooms had beds in them, of course. With Charlotte's tight leather skirt, sheer button-down, white shirt over a lacy black bra, high-heeled shoes, and hair up in a bun, she was the quintessential teacher or professor. Damn, she was so freaking sexy—on the inside and out.

"Strip, then stand and present at the foot of the bed, Michael, while I get a few things ready."

Her tone was cool and had Mike's gut roiling. He cleared his throat. "Um . . . permission to speak, Mistress?"

Standing in front of several cabinets, she glanced over her shoulder at him, her eyes narrowed. "Permission denied. I gave you an order, subbie."

His heart sank. Well, if he only had three days left on their contract, he was going to store up as many memories as he could to get him through the lonely nights that were ahead of him. "Yes, Ma'am."

Removing his jeans—he'd gone commando as instructed—he folded them neatly before placing them on a nearby chair. Stepping over to the bed with its clean sheets, he faced away from it, put his feet shoulder-width apart, clasped his forearms behind his back, bowed his head, and waited.

Charlotte opened and closed several cabinet doors and drawers, retrieving a few items, before moving about the room—all in complete silence. Finally, she stopped in front of him. "Lie down on the bed, Michael. Arms and legs spread out to the four corners."

After he complied with her order, she went to each corner of the bed and attached leather restraints to his wrists and ankles. This wasn't the first time she'd done this to him, so he was positive his anxiety didn't have anything to do with the fact he was at her utter mercy. He swallowed hard as she ensured each cuff wasn't cutting off the blood flow to his hands or feet. "Bend your knees and place your feet flat on the bed, Michael."

When he followed her command, she nodded and then turned to retrieve several items she'd left on the countertop. Moving back to the side of the bed, she showed him what was in her hands.

Oh, shit. While he'd never used one before, he immediately recognized the anal plug she held. And from the looks of it, the thing vibrated. She also had a blindfold, a bottle of lube, nipple clamps, and a cock ring. The toys were on his yellow list after she'd explained the night they'd negotiated their contract how they would amp up his orgasms during play.

"First, I'm going to decorate you, my sub, and then . . . well, I'll tell you what's next when I'm done. What's your safeword?"

"Red, Mistress."

"Very good. If you need me to slow down but not stop, use the word yellow."

"Yes, Ma'am."

Setting everything but the blindfold on the bed next to him, Charlotte stretched the elastic of the blindfold and pulled it down over his head, covering his eyes. She ran her hands over his arms, shoulders, chest, thighs, and calves, and he relaxed into her touch. He now knew what Nick had meant when he'd said Jake grounded him during a scene because that was exactly how Charlotte made Mike feel right now. He was under her spell and didn't want to be anywhere else.

Her hands left him, and the bed dipped by his feet as she climbed up between his legs. Mike moistened his suddenly dry lips but remained quiet. He heard her flip open the top to the lube. Several seconds passed before she took hold of his semi-erection and placed the cock ring over the tip, sliding it down his shaft to the root.

"The lube will help me remove it later. It should feel tight but not painful. Give me a color, Michael."

"I-I'm green, Mistress." And also getting extremely hard, the ring tightening around the base of his cock. He'd learned the ring was intended to restrict the blood flow leaving his cock after it was fully erect. The result would make his orgasm more explosive when he was finally allowed to come.

Charlotte released him, but he didn't have to wait long to find out what she planned to do next. Using the tip of the anal plug, she spread the cool lubricant over his anus. His hips bucked, and his sphincter clenched instinctively.

"Uh-uh, subbie. Relax. You've had prostate exams before with your doctor—this is no different. Well, actually, it's a helluva lot better."

"Yes, Ma'am," he responded through gritted teeth as he forced the tension from his muscles.

To his relief, she didn't immediately thrust it into him, instead slowly working the lube past the tight ring. He bit his bottom lip as he felt her exert a little pressure and then release it, each time pushing the toy a little further into his hole.

As she worked his ass, his cock hardened until he was fully erect. The ring around the base was working—it was snug enough to be just below the point of pain. He felt a drop of pre-cum ooze from his slit. It also didn't escape Charlotte's notice because the next thing he knew, she had his dick in her hand, and her tongue swiped over the tip. She took advantage of the mind-numbing distraction and plunged the plug into his ass before turning it on.

"Oh, shit!" Whatever he'd thought it would feel like didn't come close to the sensations coursing through him. The nerves in his rectum lit up, and he almost shot his load right then and there. In fact, he was sure the only thing preventing it was the cock ring.

"Clench around the plug, Michael. I can guarantee you won't like the punishment you'll receive if you lose it."

His jaw was stiff, and he breathed heavily through his nose as he tried to keep the foreign object inside him. Once again, he willed the muscles in his body to relax. After a moment, he was able to respond to her. "Yes, Mistress."

Her hand let go of the plug, leaving the round lip flush against his ass. He felt the bed dip as she crawled up his body and straddled his waist. She'd pushed her skirt up high, and the silky skin of her legs tantalized his torso. Flatting her hands, she ran them over his nipples before plucking them. They peaked under her touch as she rolled them between her fingers. He gulped when one hand left him.

"Deep breath, Michael. It will hurt a bit, but reach past the pain."

"Y-yes, Ma'am." In a flash, the rubberized tip of a clamp closed around his nipple. "Oh, fuck! Damn, that hurts!"

"Breathe, Michael." She reached back and grabbed his cock, dragging her soft hand up and down his hard flesh.

The distraction worked. His brain was quickly becoming a pile of mush. When she applied the second clamp, the pain barely registered in his mind. All he could concentrate on was where Charlotte's skin was touching his and the pleasure racing through his body, screaming at him to come.

Charlotte's nails scored his sternum. "Now that you're at my mercy and properly prepped, I believe you asked for permission to speak earlier. It is now granted. What's on that intelligent mind of yours, Michael?"

"Huh?"

"You wanted to tell me something, and you better make it quick. That cock ring can only stay on for twenty minutes. It's much easier to remove if you've already come. However, the lube will be enough to help me remove it if you haven't. I don't need to tell you which one will be more enjoyable for you."

Mike's mind was swirling. What had he wanted to say to her? It was on the tip of his tongue. "Um . . . I, uh . . . I wanted to know what will happen in a few days—when we reach the end of our contract?"

"Hmm. So that's what's been bothering you," she said as if he'd just solved a great mystery for her. "What do you want to happen, Michael?"

Her hands ran up and down his arms and torso, occasionally brushing against the clamps, sending erotic shockwaves through his nerves that seemed to go straight to his straining cock. He moaned before taking the plunge and answering her. "I-I want to renew the contract, Mistress, but I want to make some changes."

SEVENTEEN

Charlotte let out the breath she'd been holding. Her heart pounded in her chest, but she managed to keep her tone of voice from announcing that. Reaching down, she pulled off his blindfold, and he blinked his eyelids rapidly as he adjusted from going from dark to light.

She brushed her thumb across his lips. "Really? Like what?"

His gaze met hers as he inhaled deeply and let it out again slowly. "I don't want an end date, Charlotte . . . Mistress. I want to see where you and I can go from here. I know this was only supposed to be you introducing me to the lifestyle, but somewhere along the line, I . . . I fell in love with you, and I'm scared to death you don't feel the same."

Charlotte's mouth dropped open. That'd been the last thing she'd expected him to say. Going up on her knees, she put her hands on either side of his head, her face mere inches from his. "My sweet, brave sub. Is that what's been on your mind these last few days?"

"Yes, Ma'am."

Leaning down, she brushed her lips against his in the softest of kisses. "I love you too, Michael."

His breath hitched as his eyes grew wide in disbelief. "Please, say it again, Mistress."

The corners of her mouth ticked upward. "I love you too, Michael. I'd actually been planning on telling you that tonight before I got worried about why you were so quiet. You're more than just my submissive in the bedroom and my equal outside of it—you're the love my heart has been searching for—the one I never expected to find at this point in my life. I don't want an end date on our contract either, but I also don't want to rush things between us. This is all still new territory for both of us, but I'm willing to see where it leads us. You've changed me, Michael. I'd always thought I had to keep the different facets of my life separate from each other, but you've shown me how I can merge them together and still stay true to who I am."

Reaching over, she undid the strapped restraint from one of his wrists and then the other. Wrapping her fingers around his hands, she brought them to her hips. His fingers curled into her flesh. "You've brought happiness to my life, my love. I never thought I'd find someone who would give me the courage to relinquish the control I so desperately need. But you have. While it won't happen often, I like knowing I'll be able to every now and then."

When his brow narrowed in confusion, she quickly kissed him again, then looked him in the eyes. "Make me lose control, Michael. Make me scream your name."

Rising up on her knees, she shifted down on the mattress until she was above his pelvis. Mike grabbed his cock and held it upright for her. She produced a condom she'd tucked into her bra for safekeeping and swiftly put it on him. He groaned as she lowered herself onto him, her slick heat engulfing him. Clutching her waist, he jerked her downward as he thrust up into her. Charlotte gasped as his pelvic bone made contact with her clit. Leaning back, she undid the restraints around his ankles, giving him back his control. The nipple clamps were next. "Deep breath. There will be a flash of pain as the blood rushes back in."

He inhaled and then nodded. When she released the clamps together, his hips bucked again, driving him deeper inside her. "Fuck! Damn, that hurts!"

But it obviously didn't hurt enough to slow him down. Together, they lifted her and slammed her back down onto him. Mike's pace was almost frantic, and Charlotte held on for the ride. He filled her over and over.

Charlotte's climax hit her fast and hard, and she screamed his name as she tumbled into a euphoric fissure where only she, Mike, and their love existed. Her walls rippled around him. He thrust deep within her and, with a roar, stilled as her orgasm triggered his own.

Gasping for oxygen, Charlotte collapsed on top of Mike, his own heaving lungs causing her to rise and fall with every breath he took. He wrapped his arms around her and held her close. Brushing his lips against her temple, his whispered words filled her heart. "I love you, my Mistress."

THREE WEEKS LATER ...

Charlotte chuckled as Mike glared across the room. As they waited for the bartender to take their order, Charlotte curled into her lover's side and wrapped her arm around his waist. "I thought you liked the guy."

"I did until I realized he was making a move on Mom," he said, putting his arm around her shoulders as his mother and Chad Walker, a retired policeman, flirted with each other.

Chad. Just the guy's name had Mike thinking he was a

playboy and up to no good, despite a stellar thirty-year career with the New York City Police Department. He'd retired to Florida ten years ago at the age of sixty-two and moved into Twin Ponds after breaking his hip last year while riding a skateboard, of all things.

Of course, Jake had done a background check on the guy the other day after discovering he had a romantic interest in Emma.

"I think it's cute. He's quite handsome and charming."

Mike snorted in disgust before giving the bartender their order. It was Mother's Day, and the assisted living facility had thrown a really nice brunch for their residents and any guests they wanted to invite. Mike was impressed with the place, and after settling in a few weeks ago, his mother finally declared she loved it. There were plenty of activities scheduled throughout each day of the week to stimulate the residents' minds and bodies—Tai Chi, word games, arts and crafts, a walking club, a bridge club, trips to the mall or shows, and more. Emma had quickly made friends, and her old neighbor, Linda, often stopped by to visit or take her out to lunch. The only thing Mike didn't like about the place was *Chad*.

Jake wasn't faring much better in that department, and Nick enjoyed busting the brothers' asses over it. At least they'd gotten good news from Emma's doctor. Her tests for Alzheimer's had come back negative. The memory loss and confusion at times had been the result of low sodium levels. He'd put her on a new medication to stabilize it, along with a new prescription for high blood pressure. Even Emma had noticed the difference in her mental status after a week, declaring she was thinking much more clearly.

The kitchen in the house Jake and Mike had grown up in was in the process of being renovated by Parker Christiansen's company. Because of his friendship with the men, Parker had moved the job to the top of his list. As soon as there were no longer any signs of the fire and resulting damage, they were going to list it with a realtor. Mike didn't think it would take long to get an offer—it was in a great neighborhood with a nice backyard and was the perfect size for a young family.

Taking the cans of soda and water bottles the bartender had given them, Charlotte and Mike made their way back across the dining room to where the others had commandeered a table. His mother's new boyfriend and Nick were talking baseball while Jake and Emma were chatting with one of the other residents who'd stopped by their table. Mike handed out the drinks and then pulled out Charlotte's chair for her, garnering an approving smile from his mother and her friend.

When the other woman returned to her table and Chad excused himself to go to the restroom, Jake took advantage of the fact the small group was just family now and lightly rapped his knuckles on the table. "I have an announcement to make, and you're the first to know. We'll be letting Nick's family know later this afternoon. We've chosen a wedding date and location."

"Hey, that's great!" Mike slapped his brother on the back while Charlotte smiled and clapped her hands in celebration.

Emma squealed and leaned over to hug Nick, sitting beside her, before placing her hand on Jake's since he was sitting across from her. "It's about time. You have to know, Nick, that I already consider you my son-in-law, and I'm just so happy you're making it official. When and where?"

"We're renting a party boat on the Gulf . . . in two weeks. We just want our immediate family and our team there," Nick said. When he'd returned to Florida after retiring from the Navy SEALs, he'd been placed on the Alpha Team with his brothers and Jake. "That includes you, Charlotte. You're family—we expect you to be there."

She lifted her bottle of water in a toast. "I'm honored to accept."

"Two weeks!" Emma exclaimed. "We can't possibly put together a beautiful wedding in two weeks!"

Jake held up his hand. "Easy, Mom. There was a cancellation, so we put a deposit down. Nick's folks will be heading overseas the second week in June for a month with Operation Smile, and we didn't want to have the wedding in the middle of July or August—the heat would be unbearable. Besides, the yacht staff takes care of most of it."

"Oh, what do they know? We don't want some run-of-the-mill wedding—we want it done right." Her eyes cut to her other son's girlfriend. "Charlotte, you can help me. I'm sure Jenn and the Trident women will too. Nick, I'll call your mother tonight and discuss everything with her. When will they be flying in? Oh, wait—you haven't told them yet. Let me know as soon as you do. We'll need to make an assignment list. Flowers, decorations, wedding favors, a band . . . or do you want a DJ?" Without waiting for an answer, she pointed to Mike. "You can be in charge of the dinner menu and hors d'oeuvres. We'll need an open bar with tonic for your brother, Nick—I know that's what Devon prefers. And ginger ale for Angie and Fancy since they're pregnant. And, of course, Fancy will be in charge of the cake . . ."

Charlotte laughed while Mike, Jake, and Nick rolled their eyes as Emma continued her rambling. Reaching over to clasp Charlotte's hand, Mike squeezed it, earning him a peck on the cheek. He'd never get tired of touching her. What she saw in him, he had no idea, but he was grateful for every moment he had with her. They hadn't really talked about the future—marriage and kids—yet. Instead, they were taking things one special day at a time. But Mike was certain he'd found his soulmate. She was funny, beautiful, caring, and rocked his world in a way he could never have foreseen. While she dominated him in the bedroom, she was his equal every other time—and he wouldn't want it any other way.

If you're following the best reading order of the Trident Security series and its spinoffs, up next is *Cheating the Devil*, which is part of Susan Stoker's Operation Alpha World. **Available on limited sites.

If you want to read about Jake and Nick's wedding, check out the *Trident Security Field Manual*!

Also by

***Denotes titles/series that are available on select digital sites only. Paperbacks and audiobooks are available on most book sites.

THE TRIDENT SECURITY SERIES

Leather & Lace

His Angel

Waiting For Him

Not Negotiable: A Novella

Topping The Alpha

Watching From the Shadows

Whiskey Tribute: A Novella

Tickle His Fancy

No Way in Hell: A Steel Corp/Trident Security Crossover (co-authored with J.B. Havens)

Absolving His Sins

Option Number Three: A Novella

Salvaging His Soul

Trident Security Field Manual

Torn In Half: A Novella

***HEELS, RHYMES, & NURSERY CRIMES SERIES

(WITH 13 OTHER AUTHORS)
Jack Be Nimble: A Trident Security-Related Short Story

***THE DEIMOS SERIES
Handling Haven: Special Forces: Operation Alpha
Cheating the Devil: Special Forces: Operation Alpha

THE TRIDENT SECURITY OMEGA TEAM SERIES
Mountain of Evil
A Dead Man's Pulse
Forty Days & One Knight

THE DOMS OF THE COVENANT SERIES
Double Down & Dirty
Entertaining Distraction
Knot a Chance

THE BLACKHAWK SECURITY SERIES
Tuff Enough
Blood Bound

MASTER KEY SERIES
Master Key Resort
Master Cordell

HAZARD FALLS SERIES
Don't Fight It
Don't Shoot the Messenger

THE MALONE BROTHERS SERIES
Take the Money and Run

The Devil's Spare Change

LARGO RIDGE SERIES
Cold Feet

ANTELOPE ROCK SERIES
(CO-AUTHORED WITH J.B. HAVENS)
Wannabe in Wyoming
Wistful in Wyoming

AWARD-WINNING STANDALONE BOOKS
The Road to Solace
Scattered Moments in Time: A Collection of Short Stories & More

***THE BID ON LOVE SERIES
(WITH 7 OTHER AUTHORS!)
Going , Going, Gone: Book 2

***THE COLLECTIVE: SEASON TWO
(WITH 7 OTHER AUTHORS!)
Angst: Book 7

SPECIAL COLLECTIONS
Trident Security Series: Volume I
Trident Security Series: Volume II
Trident Security Series: Volume III
Trident Security Series: Volume IV
Trident Security Series: Volume V
Trident Security Series: Volume VI

About

USA Today Bestselling Author and Award-Winning Author Samantha Cole is a retired policewoman and former paramedic. Using her life experiences and training, she strives to find the perfect mix of suspense and romance for her readers to enjoy.

Awards:

Wannabe in Wyoming (co-authored by J.B. Havens) won the bronze medal in the 2021 Readers' Favorite Awards in the General Romance category.

Scattered Moments in Time, won the gold medal in the 2020 Readers' Favorite Awards in the Fiction Anthology category.

The Road to Solace (formerly *The Friar*), won the silver medal in the 2017 Readers' Favorite Awards in the Contemporary Romance category.

Samantha has over thirty-five books published throughout several different series as well as a few standalone novels. A full list can be found on her website.

Sexy Six-Pack's Sirens Group on Facebook
Website: www.samanthacoleauthor.com
Newsletter: www.geni.us/SCNews

- facebook.com/SamanthaColeAuthor
- instagram.com/samanthacoleauthor
- bookbub.com/profile/samantha-a-cole
- goodreads.com/SamanthaCole
- tiktok.com/@samanthacoleauthor

Made in the USA
Middletown, DE
30 July 2025